WHEN A COWBOY SKIPS CHRISTMAS

THE BRIDGER BUNCH

Vicki Lewis Thompson

Ocean Dance Press

Mila stepped closer, bringing her cinnamon scent with her. "What if you don't screw it up?"

"Okay, maybe that won't be the story. But what if we get into this relationship and discover we're not right for each other?"

"We'll be responsible adults." She laid her palms on his chest. "We'll admit our mistake, part friends and move on."

"You make it sound so easy." The warmth of her hands drove Cole insane, but he had to talk this through. "It wouldn't be."

"Not at first." She slid her hands up to his shoulders and lifted her face to his. "But this family's had a lot of practice in healing wounds. We'd have help. We'd be fine."

"I can be a jerk sometimes. I can't promise—"

"Neither can I. I have a temper. Ask Claudie." She gave his shoulders a slow massage. "Here's the big question. Do you want me?"

The question hit him dead center, sending waves of longing through every cell of his body. "You have no idea how much."

The McGavin Brothers
A Cowboy's Strength
A Cowboy's Honor
A Cowboy's Return
A Cowboy's Heart
A Cowboy's Courage
A Cowboy's Christmas
A Cowboy's Kiss
A Cowboy's Luck
A Cowboy's Charm
A Cowboy's Challenge
A Cowboy's Baby
A Cowboy's Holiday
A Cowboy's Choice
A Cowboy's Worth
A Cowboy's Destiny
A Cowboy's Secret
A Cowboy's Homecoming

Sons of Chance
What a Cowboy Wants
A Cowboy's Temptation
Claimed by the Cowboy
Should've Been a Cowboy
Cowboy Up
Cowboys Like Us
Count on a Cowboy
The Way to a Cowboy's Heart
Trust in a Cowboy
Only a Cowboy Will Do
Wild About the Cowboy
Cowboys and Angels
A Last Chance Christmas

1

Almost four o'clock. Any minute Mila would be coming up the outside staircase to the hayloft Cole had transformed into his living quarters.

The Bridger Bunch, especially Mila, had been supportive when he'd proposed the conversion last July. By using every spare moment, he'd pulled it off before the first snowfall.

He'd insulated the hell out of the space to counteract critter noise from below and severe weather from outside. Now that another Montana winter was in full swing and the horses stayed indoors quite a bit, he could claim victory on both counts.

Triple-pane windows and four skylights added views and airiness throughout the day. But at this hour in December, he lowered the shades and turned on all six of his hanging lanterns to create a welcoming glow.

Mila hadn't been up here since he'd given the family a tour in October. No one had. Once the loft had been basically finished, he'd started work on his secret project. Now he was ready to show it off, and he'd chosen Mila as the first to see what he'd created.

The animatronic display at the Rockin' Racoon had captured his imagination back in July. Two months ago he'd made an appointment with Clem, the tavern's owner, to get the schematics for the control panel and the wiring. He'd made numerous notes and taken countless pictures.

Thank goodness for online supply sources and Clem's patience. The guy had cheerfully answered a million texts. Evidently he was tickled to have another animatronics geek in town.

Two days ago Cole had contacted Mila to set up this visit. He'd thrown a sheet over it so he could give her a brief explanation before the big reveal.

If she liked what he'd done, it would pass muster with the others. They valued her opinion, and in the six months he'd lived at Laughing Creek Ranch, he'd come to value it, too.

But it was more than that. He wanted to impress her. There it was, his hidden agenda. He had a crush.

Because she hadn't been up here in weeks, he'd put elbow grease into tidying up. His place looked fudging good, if he did say so, especially with that round electric fireplace.

He'd blown a chunk of his budget on that red beauty, which hung from a twelve-foot black pipe attached to the rafters. Its 360-degree view of the realistic flames had inspired his open floor plan.

If he pushed back the sliding barn doors that closed off his bedroom, he could enjoy the dancing light and warmth from his bed. This afternoon the doors were closed.

He'd added them in November, after the family tour. They changed the feel of the space from studio apartment to sexy hideaway. At least he thought so, especially when the open doors framed a view of his king-sized bed. But he hadn't created that vibe on purpose.

Or maybe he had. In any case, his invitation to Mila wasn't a come-see-my-etchings seduction routine. Not the Cole Sterling way.

Had he fantasized her sharing his bed? Sure. Who could blame him? She was gorgeous, smart and kind-hearted. She had an interest in him, too, judging from quite a few warm glances she'd aimed in his direction.

They'd had slow-burn chemistry from day one. Hadn't done anything about it, although they'd flirted a bit at his sister Jordan's wedding to Luis in October. At Jordie's urging, Cole had brought his fiddle to the reception.

He'd sat in with the band and done a few solos. Soon folks started making requests for tunes he didn't know. Mila to the rescue. If she could hum it, he could play it and she'd sing along. They'd had fun teaming up.

But he hadn't made a move. Neither had she. Soon after the wedding, this animatronic endeavor had sucked up his free time. She'd teased him about his mysterious project, clearly hoping he'd let her in on it. Not a chance.

He hadn't dared let anyone know other than Clem. The possibility of failure had ridden his ass every step of the way. But damned if he hadn't managed to build something that made him laugh.

That was promising, but not enough. He wanted it to entertain other people. Especially Mila.

That said, getting involved with her was risky. She was literally the boss's daughter. Not that losing his job as Laughing Creek's handyman was a big deal. He was highly employable and he knew it.

The risk was strictly emotional. He'd fallen head-over-heels for this ranch, this family. Because they'd generously allowed him to modify the hayloft any way he chose, he had his first real home.

And his own horse. The sleek chestnut who'd been wild until Luis and Rio had coaxed him into the training barn toward the end of July was now gentle enough for a kid to ride.

When Cole had tried to buy him, Luis had shocked him by offering Sparky as a gift. Turned out he and Rio had intended that animal for Cole all along, which was why he'd been named Sparky, fitting for a master electrician.

He glanced at his wall clock. Four o'clock on the dot. Was she on her way? His soundproofing kept him from hearing her boots on the metal stairs outside.

Might as well take a look. Tugging on his boots, he opened the door and stuck his head out. A blast of cold air slapped him in the face. Yep, there she was, about a third of the way up, head down, the hood of her red parka covering her dark curls.

His heart rate spiked. Stepping out on the landing, he grabbed the railing as his boots skidded on newly formed ice. "Be careful! It's slippery."

"*Si, amigo.*" Gripping the metal rail with one gloved hand, she clutched a potted evergreen with the other. "These stairs are *no bueno*, especially in winter." Her breath produced little puffs of fog. "You should install an elevator."

"Or enclose the staircase."

"I can't believe you suffer through this whenever you visit Sparky."

"It's not so bad with a coat on."

She glanced up. "Where's your coat now? What are you doing standing outside like a moron? Go back in!"

"I'm fine." He hunched his shoulders to keep from shivering. "Looks like I'm getting a gift."

"You probably have a big tree already."

"No, ma'am."

"Good thing I brought this, then. We've got less than a week left."

"Guess so."

"Sneaks up on you."

"That's a fact." *Christmas.* He'd been so busy he'd mostly blocked the evidence it was approaching. He'd probably deploy his usual tactic — pretending to have a highly contagious cold on the twenty-third that conveniently lasted for three days.

The tree was a sweet gesture, though. Looked like she might have decorated it herself. She had no way of knowing how much he dreaded the holiday. "Let me take that." He reached for it as she neared the top step.

"Okay." She handed it over and finished the climb, breathing fast. "Now get the hell inside."

"After you." He gestured toward the open door.

With a resigned sigh, she ducked in, toed off her boots on the mat and moved aside to make room for him. "You'd better not get sick."

"I won't." Fudge it all. Now when he pretended to be sick, she'd be put out with him for standing in the cold waiting for her. Oh, well. Couldn't be helped now.

Closing the door, he shucked his boots, carried the tree to the kitchen island and set it down. "Great decorating job."

"Thanks." She flipped back her hood and unzipped her coat. "I adore trimming trees." She tucked her gloves in her coat pockets. "You'll have to come see all the ones Claudie and I put up."

"Love to." He'd ignore the trees and concentrate on her. The mini-hacienda she shared with her sister was a short walk away, but he'd only been there a couple of times. Playing it cool.

"I tied the ornaments on tight, so you don't have to worry about things falling off." Shrugging out of her coat, she hung it on a peg by the door. She'd worn a white sweater with a green wreath on the front.

He pushed down a wave of anxiety. "Smells great." So did she, a spicy scent he didn't remember noticing before. Cinnamon? Fortunately he didn't connect the scent to the holiday, or the aroma of evergreens, either.

But once ornaments hung from the branches, they turned into something he regularly avoided. He'd cut Christmas out of his life the minute he'd left his parents' house at sixteen. When he and Jordan had shared an apartment, December twenty-fifth had been just another day. By mutual agreement.

"After the ground unfreezes, you can plant it." Mila headed toward the island, her sock feet whispering over the wood floor.

"Is there a certain spot on the property where it should go?"

"There is. We had a pine beetle infestation years ago and had to clear out a section of forest. We planted seedlings that spring, and now we add any live trees we buy at Christmas. I'll go with you. I have a couple of these small ones, too."

"It's a deal." His pulse rate picked up. She was within arm's reach. Had they ever been completely alone like this? Not that he could remember.

Judging from the flicker of awareness in her brown eyes, she'd had the same realization. Turning away, she surveyed the area. "Your place looks inviting on a cold winter day."

"Thanks." Not as inviting as she looked. He shoved his hands in his pockets. Technically her Christmas-themed sweater should neutralize his urge to touch her. It didn't.

She pointed to the far end of the space. "I assume the surprise is under that sheet."

"It is." With luck, the animatronics would distract him from the hot thoughts swirling in his brain.

"Did you have those barn doors when we were all here in October?"

"Just got them last month. I saw the idea online and liked it." Thank God he'd followed his instincts and left them closed. He wasn't ready to throw caution to the winds.

"They look great. I'll bet you open them at night, though."

"I do." He headed toward the animatronics. Time to switch subjects.

She followed him over. "Figured you'd want to open the doors so you can see the fireplace."

His breath caught. Was she imagining how the fire would look from his bed? The implications stirred him up more than a little.

She wandered toward the sliding doors. "Then again, it might not matter. You probably turn the flame off."

Alrighty. If she wanted to talk about this, he'd go along. "As a matter of fact, it does matter. I like watching the flames before I go to sleep. They're on a timer that clicks off at midnight." Hooking his thumbs in his belt-loops, he acted like this loaded topic didn't affect him at all.

"As I recall, it's a nice-looking bed."

He almost swallowed his tongue. Really? She was going there? He hadn't planned to seduce her, but what if she'd planned to seduce him?

She turned back in his direction. "I'd be inclined to leave the doors partway open even in the daytime."

"Would you, now?" He held her gaze, searching for clues in her warm brown eyes.

"I think it would make the space look bigger."

"It's an idea." Several other ideas came to him. They started with opening the barn doors. He might not be ready to make this move, but what if she was? Would he insult her by not picking up on her cues?

"Unless you never make your bed."

"I usually do." Maybe he should fudging kiss her and take the guesswork out of it. He moved a step in her direction. For months he'd dreamed of tasting her full mouth and feeling the sweet press of her—

"Okay, I get it." Cheeks rosy, she flashed him a smile.

He froze, thrown off his game by that big ol' smile. "Get what?"

"You have one set of sheets and you pulled off the top one to cover your surprise, which means your bed's a hot mess right now."

It wasn't. The sheet over the animatronics was an old one, but now he was second-guessing his decision to kiss her. He might have misinterpreted this bedroom discussion.

"Don't mind me. The doors look terrific and they add a level of privacy. That must be nice." She broke eye contact and glanced around. "I just realized you don't have any Christmas decorations."

"Yes, I do." He was confused. Now she sounded flustered. He gestured toward the little tree. "A nice person brought me that."

"But your dramatic fireplace just cries out for...oh, wait. I keep forgetting single guys don't tend to decorate much."

Yeah, she was nervous, all right. And trying to cover it with chatter.

"My brothers would probably just get a tree and call it good, except now they're required to go all in."

He'd help her out. "Why?" Good thing he hadn't kissed her. Even if she'd wanted him to, she was clearly conflicted about it. Now she seemed determined to discuss holiday décor.

"Grandma and the aunties left boxes of decorations when they turned over their houses to my brothers and they expect to see everything put up. They have standards."

"I'm sure." He got a kick out of those four women—the Dazzling Damsels. They did their best to live up to the name they'd chosen.

But inserting those spunky ladies into the conversation indicated Mila was backing off. She might have briefly toyed with the idea of getting jiggy, but if so, she'd chickened out. Just as well.

"That's the main reason you see wreaths on doors and lights strung up outside their houses."

"Oh." Technically he hadn't seen anything. He was an expert at directing his attention elsewhere.

"Well, that goes for the bachelors. Adam and Tracy put theirs up together and Luis might have decorated more for Jordan than to please Auntie Carmen this year."

"Maybe." He doubted his sister had been the driver of that activity. But he'd had very few chances to talk privately with her recently. She might have been able to ditch her negative associations and enjoy her first Christmas with the Bridger Bunch.

"You've probably noticed that Mom and Greta go big for the holiday, too."

"Yes, ma'am." A tiny white lie. No one, not even Jordie, knew how much Christmas triggered him. He wanted it to stay that way.

"Anyway, I've rattled on long enough. Can I please see this secret of yours?"

"Absolutely." His original excitement for the project helped center him. He crossed to the sheet-draped display. "But before I take this off, I have a disclaimer. I had fun making what you're about to see, but if you think it won't work for the family, I'll just use it to amuse myself."

"Does it amuse you?"

"Well, yeah, but—"

"Then there's an excellent chance I'll love it. Let's take a look."

"Alrighty." An unexpected touch of stage fright made him hesitate. Then he reached for the sheet and yanked it off.

"Oh, my gosh!" Her bright laughter spilled out and her eyes sparkled with delight. "Beavers! Three adorable beavers!"

"Yes, ma'am." Relief flooded through him and he grinned. "It's the Beaver Bunch."

2

Mila had never seen something so clever and appealing in her life. By creating it, this big tough cowboy had just added a whole new dimension to his captivating personality.

"Cole, I love it." And she hugged him. A split second after she'd thrown her arms around his muscular torso she reconsidered that impulse and stepped back. "Sorry. I got carried away."

His gaze was direct. "No apologies necessary."

The light in his gray eyes made her quiver. Her breasts tingled from the momentary press of his solid chest and her nose was totally enjoying the scent of his aftershave. The sound of his quick breath echoed in her ears.

What was wrong with her? She couldn't seem to stop sending mixed signals. She'd promised herself this was only a social call, but within minutes she'd stumbled into an ill-advised conversation about his bedroom that had almost gotten her kissed.

After diffusing that situation, she'd landed back in the soup by giving him a spontaneous hug. If she didn't figure out her intentions toward Cole

Sterling in the next few seconds, her wayward libido was liable to make the decision for her.

"I like you, Mila."

His husky confession sent flames licking through her body. "I like you, too."

"Want to see how it works?"

She gasped. "Now?"

His eyebrows rose. Then he chuckled.

The sound of that chuckle, low and sexy as hell, doused her with lust. Was he about to make a move? Was she?

"I was talking about this." He gestured toward the animatronics. "But if you want to talk about something else, then—"

"Nope!" She snapped out of her hormone-drenched fantasy. "I knew that's what you meant."

He didn't contradict her. Not out loud. But his knowing glance said it all.

For months she'd kept her feelings under control, sensing his hesitancy toward getting involved. That had been easy since they were never alone. Then he'd buried himself in this project.

But now...they were so alone. Completely, arousingly alone. Her heart pounded like crazy. She'd seriously underestimated the effect that would have on her.

He took a breath. "I swear I didn't ask you up here to seduce you."

"I'm sure you didn't."

"Why are you sure?"

"That's not you, *amigo*." She swallowed, tried to marshal her thoughts. "You've been super respectful. Ambivalent, too."

"Because I am."

"For the record, I didn't come up here with ulterior motives."

"But here we are." His warm gaze searched hers. "We should probably have a conversation about it."

"We should. Definitely." A discussion? That option hadn't crossed her mind.

"But first I need to cool down. And I'd like to show you these guys in action."

"I'd like that, too." She barely had enough breath to speak. He needed to cool down after one hug? Wow.

"Then here goes." He walked over to a control box on the wall to the left of the platform.

Drawing in air, she released it slowly. They'd acknowledged what had been simmering between them for months. Was she ready to go forward?

Cole had switched his attention to his project, giving her a moment to calm down, too. *Or* she could spend the time imagining the wonders hidden beneath his loose-fitting clothes. She chose Option B.

How would it feel being held by arms strong enough to carry a stack of planks from his truck to the loft? To have his capable hands stroke her in intimate places? To touch his broad chest, to cup glutes made firm by all those trips up and down the stairs, to cradle—

"I timed their motions to a recording from a jug band I played with a few years ago."

"A jug band? You were in a jug band?" The question came out as a high-pitched squeak.

He turned to face her, his gray eyes sparkling with amusement. "That surprises you?"

"Not really. I mean... I shouldn't be. You play a mean fiddle." *Get it together, girlfriend.*

"Thanks." He accepted the compliment easily without a trace of arrogance.

Well, he should be proud of his abilities. After all, excellence was his trademark.... That realization inspired another wave of lust.

Obviously he was aware. His gray eyes momentarily darkened. With an almost imperceptible shake of his head, he turned back toward the trio of beavers. "The circular platform they're on is designed to rotate so the whole display moves outside to sit above the barn doors."

"Wow. That's cool."

"It is if it works. Haven't tested it yet."

"Why not?" She would by damn pay attention to what he'd created. He'd honored her by letting her see it before anyone else.

"I'd have to do it at night to preserve the surprise and in this weather it might get stuck."

"I guess it could. So you'll only rotate it outside during the day in the winter?"

"I'll have to see how it goes, weather-wise. It's designed to look good at night, too. Here's phase one, the static display." He flicked a switch and several small lanterns glowed on the knotty pine wall of the rustic country bandstand. Footlights illuminated the performers.

She sighed with pleasure. "That's beautiful."

"I wanted it to be interesting whether they're playing or not." He studied his little critters with obvious affection. "On a warm summer evening, they can be out there looking cute even when they're not doing anything."

"And if the weather's bad, you can bring them back in. Brilliant."

"Weather was the critical problem I had to solve. I knew they could sit on the overhang above the barn doors, but unlike the raccoons over the bar, they can't stay there."

"But they can perform in here, instead."

He smiled. "If you mean I just created the perfect party venue—"

"You sure did. Especially if they can play more than one song."

"They can."

She glanced back at the couch and easy chairs surrounding the fireplace. "And here I thought you might be a bit of a recluse."

"What gave you that idea?"

"You soundproofed this loft as if you were making a recording studio. Or a man cave."

He laughed. "Never wanted a man cave. But I would like the horses and me to be good neighbors who don't disturb each other. That doesn't make me a hermit."

"I see your point, but you also seemed perfectly happy tucked away for two months working on your secret project."

"I was, but mostly because I was excited about getting this done. I also have a great time hanging out with your family."

"We're not too much?"

"Not at all. I'm fine with this becoming a party venue because I'm also pretty good at telling people when the party's over. But performing in here isn't the goal. I need this platform to rotate or the plan's a bust."

"Well, either the mechanism works or you'll figure out how to fix it. That's what my dad always said about his projects."

"Judging from what I've heard, that guy was a genius."

"Who says you're not?"

That clearly startled him. Then his expression changed and his eyes gleamed the way they had when she'd been carrying on about the barn doors. "Watch your language, lady." He adopted a lazy drawl. "Them's kissin' words."

A flood of desire almost left her speechless. Almost. She lifted her chin and met his intense gaze. "So what?"

His soft laughter rippled over her like a caress. "We've come this far. I'll be damned if I'm gonna fudging kiss you before I show you how these varmints perform."

"Then you'd better turn them on quick, *amigo*." Her words came out in a breathless rush, as a courage she didn't know she had made her bold. "We're running out of time."

"Yes, ma'am. It does look that way." Facing the control box again, he hit another switch.

The animals came to life — slapping their tails in rhythm on the floor and playing their instruments — a fiddle, a washboard and a washtub string bass.

All God's Creatures Got a Place in the Choir poured from speakers mounted on the platform. The bass player and the percussionist appeared to sing along. The fiddler kept up a lively motion with his bow. The charming performance brought a unexpected lump to her throat. Her dad would have loved this.

"Mila?"

She glanced up.

The music had ended and Cole stood close, very close, his brow furrowed. "Is something wrong with it?"

"No, it's beautiful, stupendous, incredible."

"But you look sad."

"Because my dad would've gone nuts over those furry creatures. He would have laughed so hard at calling them the Beaver Bunch. They would have brought him so much joy."

With a soft sigh and a murmured *come here,* he drew her gently into his arms.

She went gladly, gratefully, her gaze locked with his. "Didn't you want to talk first?"

"It'll have to wait."

3

Kissing Mila without clarifying...well, anything...could be a mistake. Cole accepted that possibility.

Near as he could tell, she needed a hug. It so happened he needed a kiss. Combining the two was a natural pairing.

With her breasts pressed firmly against his chest, he couldn't separate the crazy beating of his heart from hers. He held her gaze, made brighter by the color suffusing her cheeks.

She hadn't grabbed onto him yet. Her hands rested on his shoulders. Neutral. Uncommitted. To be on the safe side, he gave her time to push him away.

She stayed put, her rosy lips slightly parted, her breathing quick and shallow. Keeping her tucked close, he cupped the back of her head.

Her hair felt glorious, soft and silky. Spreading his fingers, he sifted through those dark, glossy waves.

Her breath hitched and she gripped his shoulders.

"Second thoughts?"

"Nope."

"Alrighty, then." Pulse racing, he dipped his head and touched down on her tempting mouth. Fire coursed through his veins, but he'd go slow, be gentle, not rush—

Whoa! Clearly Mila had other plans. Wrapping her arms around his neck, she urged him closer and boldly invited him in. Her whimper of impatience sent a potent message. *Take whatever you want.*

And oh, how he wanted. He deepened the kiss, plunging his tongue into her mouth. Her sexy moan blew a hole in every good intention. Gripping her tush, her pulled her in tight, groaning as his heat melded with hers.

His cock surged to life and hunger laid waste to restraint. Reaching under her sweater, he found the back catch of her bra. She moaned again, clearly urging him on. He dealt with the hooks, loosening the bra so he could cradle her breast and stroke her nipple until it grew rigid, eager for the tug of his mouth.

Her warm skin against his palm made him dizzy with anticipation. Once they made it through those barn doors, he would caress her until she begged for what they both wanted, what they'd waited for....

His better angel murmured something in his ear. He blocked it. The warning came again. *You waited for a reason, idiot! You could ruin everything!*

Mustering what little control he had left, he forced himself to stop kissing her, but he couldn't make himself let go of her breast. He gulped for air. "We have to—"

"Open the...open the doors. I know." She gasped out the words.

"First...first we should...talk."

"Talk?" Panting, she wiggled out of his arms, dislodging his hand. "Now?"

"Yes." He fought the urge to reach for her. "About our—"

"You had your hand on my tata!" She tugged down her sweater.

"I only meant to kiss you."

"Seriously?"

"Kissing's a big deal! A first step! I thought we'd kiss and maybe cuddle and then...talk."

She glanced at his crotch before returning her attention to his face, eyebrows lifting.

"I can't help that. You get to me."

Crossing her arms over her chest, she heaved a sigh. "*Que loco, hombre.*"

He scrubbed a hand through his hair. "Yes, ma'am. I should've known better."

Amusement flashed in her eyes and she pressed her lips together as if trying not to smile.

"To be fair, I've never kissed you. Or hugged you. We haven't even danced together."

"We line danced together."

"Doesn't count. I've never touched your body with my body."

"Well, you have now." The slight tremble of her mouth and a quiver in her speech confirmed it. She was ready to bust out laughing. "What do you think?"

"It was fudging awesome."

She grinned, her brown eyes sparkling. "Yeah."

"I want to do it again."

"I'd like that."

"But before we do, I need to find out how you see things."

Her gaze swept to his crotch again, which was still making a statement. "I see things as very promising."

His pride and joy gave her a noticeable response. Of course. She had power over that part of his anatomy now. Likely more than he did.

She looked up and smiled. "Sorry. I got distracted. What did you want to talk about?"

"Our situation. I'm the hired hand and you're the boss's daughter. We're not on equal footing."

Her blink of confusion was followed by a quick frown. "Yes, we are."

"No, we're not. I'm here because your mother hired me. You're here because you belong in this family and always will." Stating that truth cooled his jets. "If you get mad at me, or for that matter if anybody here gets upset with my behavior, I could be fired. Sent away."

Her eyes widened and her body tensed. "Did someone tell you that? Because I can't imagine—"

"No one told me. It's just the way it is."

"Ah." Her expression relaxed. "You had me going for a minute. I couldn't believe any of us would have said such a thing." Her warm gaze settled on him. "That might be the way it is in other places, but here? No."

"What do you mean?"

"You're way more than *the hired hand* as you put it. For one thing, you're my sister-in-law's brother."

"True, but that doesn't make me—"

"Actually it does. When Jordan married Luis, you became part of the Bridger Bunch whether you like it or not."

The possibility stunned him.

"You didn't figure that out?"

"No." He dragged in a breath, his chest tight with emotion. "No, I didn't."

"I guess we all thought it was obvious so nobody said it out loud. The focus was on those two, and... I'm sorry, Cole. Somebody should have made a point of it. For sure my dad would've."

He still couldn't get his head around it. "Then you're saying...."

"We're on equal footing."

"Because of my sister?"

"That clinches it, but simply living and working here makes you way more than an employee. You're one of us. There's no hierarchy at Laughing Creek, no power structure. We all pitch in. We all collect paychecks."

"Even your grandma and aunties?"

She laughed. "They could if they needed to, but those ladies are the savviest investors you'll ever meet. Mom and Adam rely on them. If you want a stock tip, knock on their door."

"I might." He took a breath. "So just by being here, I've become one of you?"

"Yes."

Stuffing his hands in his pockets, he studied the gleaming wood floor under his boots.

He could have this place with the Bridger Bunch forever? No matter what? Their display of generosity was overwhelming.

"Cole? Is that a problem?"

He met her gaze. "That makes this—" His gesture included both of them. "Riskier than ever."

"Why?"

"I was worried I'd screw it up and get kicked out. Now I'm terrified I'll screw it up and disappoint the good folks who've been nothing but kind to me."

She stepped closer, bringing her cinnamon scent with her. "What if you don't screw it up?"

"Okay, maybe that won't be the story. But what if we get into this relationship and discover we're not right for each other?"

"We'll be responsible adults." She laid her palms on his chest. "We'll admit our mistake, part friends and move on."

"You make it sound so easy." The warmth of her hands drove him insane, but he had to talk this through. "It wouldn't be."

"Not at first." She slid her hands up to his shoulders and lifted her face to his. "But this family's had a lot of practice in healing wounds. We'd have help. We'd be fine."

"I can be a jerk sometimes. I can't promise—"

"Neither can I. I have a temper. Ask Claudie." She gave his shoulders a slow massage. "Here's the big question. Do you want me?"

The question hit him dead center, sending waves of longing through every cell of his body. "You have no idea how much."

"Enough to take a risk?"

Heart pounding, he absorbed the challenge in her eyes. "Yes."

"When?"

"Now." Sweeping her into his arms, he carried her over to the barn doors and nudged them apart with his foot.

She clung to him, breathing fast as she glanced toward his massive king. "Your bed isn't a hot mess."

"It's about to be."

4

Mila gazed up at Cole, dazzled by his transformation from hesitant to all in. "That's more like it."

"Glad you approve." He set her back on her feet, pulled her close and leaned down to nuzzle her neck as he reached for the hem of her sweater. "I hope you're not expected back home anytime soon. If we do this right, it'll take a while."

Moist heat settled in her core. "I didn't... I didn't specify..." She lost track of what she was trying to say, lost in an erotic haze created by his lips moving over her skin, his close-cropped beard softer than it looked.

Slowly he drew her sweater up. Cool air touched her bare back. "Lift your arms," he murmured against her ear.

She obeyed, and he pulled off her sweater and her bra in one smooth movement.

Tossing both aside, he stepped back, "Ah, Mila." His chest heaved. "Glorious Mila. You honor me."

The need simmering in his gray eyes made her bold. Holding his gaze, she closed the gap and reached for the metal button at his waist. "Let's get this party started."

His eyes darkened to the color of rain clouds. "Be my guest." His voice rasped in the stillness.

Heart beating so loud her ears buzzed, she unfastened the button and tried to lower the zipper. Not easy, considering the strain it was under.

As she gently tugged, making very little progress, it occurred to her she'd never offered to unzip the fly of a fully aroused man. She didn't want to hurt him in the process of—

"Mila." His hands covered hers. "You're fudging gonna make me come."

She sucked in a breath and let go of the zipper tab. "Okay, you do it."

"I'll make you a deal. I'll take off mine while you take off yours."

"Okay. And your shirt."

"Yes, ma'am." He quickly unfastened a few buttons and stripped off his shirt.

The sudden reveal of his muscular pecs and sexy chest hair so thoroughly grabbed her attention that she couldn't do anything but stare. She'd figured he'd look good but damn, not this good.

"Something wrong?"

"Oh, no." She let out a sigh of delight. "Things are *muy bueno.*"

"You're falling behind." He pulled off both socks and reached for his zipper.

"I'd rather watch you."

"No problem." Pushing down his briefs along with his jeans, he kicked them away and came toward her. "I'm happy to take over."

She managed to nod in response, but she'd lost the power of speech. Not the type to draw attention to his body, Cole favored loose-fitting shirts and jeans. She'd had to guess at the wonders he'd kept covered.

Logically he'd be muscular because of the physical work he did. But that didn't necessarily translate into the kind of classic beauty standing inches away from her. What a privilege.

He paused. "If you're rethinking this, you'd better say so now."

"Just—" She cleared her throat. "Just the opposite." She met his gaze. "Why did we wait so long?"

Closing the gap, he wrapped her in his arms, his chest hair tickling her sensitized skin, his stiff cock pressing against the fabric of her jeans. "Because we're cautious people." Leaning down, he dropped a soft kiss on her mouth while shifting his hips so he could unfasten her jeans.

He was right. And she was through being cautious. Sliding her arms around him, she ran her hands over the sculpted contours of his back, thrilling to the hitch in his breathing and the ripple of his skin as he responded to her touch.

She wanted to drive him crazy and be driven crazy in return. When she squeezed his ass he thrust his tongue into her mouth with a deep groan.

Giving her jeans a tug, he got them down to her knees. She pulled one leg out and then the other. Gone.

His breathing ragged, he slipped his hands under the elastic of her panties, spread his fingers over her tush and lifted her up against the hard length of his cock. Only a thin layer of cotton separated her from what she craved. She wrapped one leg around his thigh, tightening the connection.

He broke away from the kiss, gasping. "Bedtime." Picking her up, he laid her on the quilt and yanked off her panties, throwing them over his shoulder.

Only then did she remember they needed a certain item to complete this episode. "You'd better have condoms."

"If I didn't, we wouldn't be naked. Give me a sec."

She watched him head for the bathroom, that view almost as spectacular as the one he'd treated her to moments ago. Was it too soon to ask if she could move in?

The outrageous thought made her grin. She wouldn't ask, of course. He might not be a hermit but he had strong boundaries. So did she. Like he'd said, they were cautious people.

But *Dios mio*, this was glorious. Lifting up, she pulled the quilt out from under her and pushed it to the foot of the bed.

But all the banging around in the bathroom cupboards didn't bode well. Yes, they could fool around and definitely would if they didn't have that critical component, but fooling around wasn't nearly as satisfying as—

"Found 'em!"

"*Bueno!*" Clearly he hadn't planned on seducing her or he would have had condoms at the ready.

"Don't know how the fudging things ended up in the back of a cupboard full of TP rolls." He stomped back in with a dented box.

"You'd better check to see if they're expired."

"Don't have to. Bought these right before I left Helena."

"Optimistic of you."

"Symbolic. When I bought 'em, I made myself a promise."

"Oh?"

As he approached the bed, he opened the box. Then he glanced at her. "No more meaningless sex."

The intensity in his gray eyes made her quiver. "I see."

"Maybe I should have mentioned that." Continuing to hold her gaze, he tore open the foil package and rolled on the condom.

She swallowed. "You didn't have to."

"Good." He climbed in and moved over her without breaking eye contact. "I'm not looking for a fling."

She almost couldn't hear him over the loud beat of her heart. "Me, either."

Slowly he lowered his body until his chest brushed her nipples. The tip of his cock nudged gently at the entrance to her womb, but didn't penetrate.

She absorbed the heat in his gaze and the eagerness in his ragged breathing. He wanted her, no doubt about it. But underneath that fiery need lay a deeper emotion.

She wrapped him in her arms. "You're safe with me, *cielo.*"

With a deep groan of surrender, he plunged deep.

She sucked in a breath and let it out in a long sigh of pleasure. *This.*

<u>5</u>

Cole held very still. His body demanded more, but he waited, allowing the glow in Mila's brown eyes to reach his soul. *You're safe with me.*

How had she known the answer to his unspoken question? Could he believe her?

She wrapped him in her arms and matched her breathing to his, creating delicious friction as her tight nipples grazed his chest with each inhale. This felt so incredibly right it scared him.

If he didn't know better, he'd think he'd been here before, surrounded by the scent of cinnamon, tantalized by the warmth of her thighs, cradled by her hips and awed by how perfectly their bodies fit together.

"Feels pretty good, *amigo.*"

Her murmured words made him smile. "Understatement." Leaning down, he touched his mouth to hers, then nibbled on her plump lower lip. "You're like a rich dessert. I'll have to pace myself. Take small bites."

"Sounds like fun."

"With luck it will be." Lifting his head, he watched her eyes darken as he began to move. Clearly she liked that rhythm. So did his cock, which threatened to put a quick end to this adventure. He paused. "Seems I'm too fudging sensitive."

"Or I'm too fudging hot."

He chuckled. "That, too." He dialed it back, hoping a lazy stroke would cool him down. No dice. His cock had never been this determined to go for broke only minutes into the action.

Mila's sexy response wasn't helping. She was the lover of his dreams, rising to meet him, welcoming each thrust. She made him feel like he was the lover of *her* dreams.

He desperately wanted to keep from coming, and every second brought him closer to the brink. Why couldn't he hold back?

Panting, he shoved in tight and stopped moving, his jaw clenched against the pressure pushing him to let go. "Can you stay?"

She dragged in a breath. "Stay?'

"Longer. So...so we can...do this again."

Clearly confused, she stared at him, her breasts rising and falling as she gulped in air.

"My control's shot. I don't want to come so soon, but I can't—"

"Yes!" She made a sound that was part laughter and part cry of frustration. "I'll stay! Now go for it!"

He accepted that invitation. No more tiny bites. If he'd feared the wild, raw pace would shock her, he needn't have worried. She rode the whirlwind with him, her cries blending with his as they raced toward a glittering finale.

She came first, a gift he barely had time to register before his climax hurled him into a world of blinding light and explosive sensations stronger than he'd ever known. He bowed his head as the tremors rocked him and left him dripping with sweat.

He managed not to fall on Mila even though his arm muscles ached from the effort. Bad enough that he was raining on her.

Slowly lifting his head, he met her round-eyed gaze. "You okay?"

"Are you fudging kidding me?"

"You're not okay?" Damn it, if he'd hurt her he might have to kill himself.

"I'm ten times better than okay." She reached up and wiped the sweat off his beard. "Twenty times better. I'm okay to the hundredth power."

"Oh." He smiled. Couldn't help it. He was proud of himself. "That's nice to hear. I mean, that wasn't a very long—"

"Obviously it was long enough."

"I was worried you wouldn't be able to come."

"I was worried you were going to stop and go make a sandwich or something."

"Make a sandwich?" He started laughing, an interesting experience when he was still securely tucked in.

"When asked if I could stay so we could do this again, I figured you wanted to end the current session. Like maybe you left something on the stove."

"I suppose it was a strange question."

"You have no idea. And on top of it, if you were worried that this first time would be a bust and you'd need a do-over, I'm here to tell you it was definitely not a bust. You don't need a do-over."

"Then you aren't going to stay?"

"Oh, no, I'm staying. Only an idiot would pack up and leave when there's time on the clock and a box of fresh condoms. But you should probably invite me to dinner so I have something to tell Claudie."

He grinned. He'd seen her playful side plenty of times, but now she was deliberately playing with *him*. He loved it. "Will you have dinner with me?"

"*Si, amigo.*" She batted her eyelashes. "*Gracias.* Do you have food?"

"Nothing interesting."

"No problem. I'm not here for the food."

"You're adorable."

"So are you."

He rolled his eyes.

"You *are*. You created that fabulous Beaver Bunch in secret to surprise my family on Christmas. If that's not adorable, I don't know what is."

He hadn't thought about the timing. Whoops. "I didn't mean for it to be a—"

"Maybe not when you couldn't predict how long it would take, but look how perfectly it worked out."

"Guess so." He gave her a quick kiss. "I need to go wash up. Then we can see what's in the fridge for dinner."

"You want to eat first?"

"Probably should while we're thinking about it." The moment he left the warmth of her body, he craved her all over again. He could easily forget food altogether. "And you need to call Claudie." He climbed out of bed.

"I just remembered I didn't bring my phone."

"You can use mine." He headed for the bathroom. "I'll get it in a minute."

"I'll just snuggle in and watch the fire."

"Please do." He stepped into the bathroom and glanced at the lucky cuss in the mirror. Mila Bridger had just made love with him.

He dealt with the condom and turned on the water so he could wash up. What if he hadn't found that box? Hiding it behind the TP made no sense.

Although it might if he'd been trying to keep himself from making this move. But she'd convinced him it wouldn't affect his relationship with her family, no matter how things turned out.

He wanted to believe that. She should know after living here since she was five, when Spence Bridger had become the man she called dad.

He wished he'd known the guy Mila revered so much. Spence sounded like the kind of role model he'd searched for his entire life.

When he walked back into the bedroom, Mila was sitting at the foot of his bed wearing her sweater and jeans.

She gave him a smile. "I dressed for dinner."

"Wouldn't need to. I pulled down all the shades."

"I noticed. But I don't tend to strut around naked. If you do, don't let me stop you."

"I don't strut around naked, either." He walked over to his dresser. "But under the circumstances, I'd rather wear sweats than jeans." Pulling out a pair, he stepped into them and tied the drawstring.

"Going commando, I see."

"Yes, ma'am. More efficient." He tugged on a sweatshirt.

"I left off my bra. For efficiency." She flashed him.

He sucked in a breath. "You're playing with fire, lady."

"So are you, going commando and bragging about efficiency. Now my panties are wet again."

"Oh, really?" He approached the bed. "Let's see." And he pounced.

She squealed but didn't push him away. "What do you think you're doing?"

"Verifying the state of your panties." Straddling her and pinning her down with his chest, he left room to get his hand on her jeans. "Gonna stop me?"

Her eyes glittered. "No."

"Good." He unfastened the button and pulled down the zipper. "Because you were asking for this." Damn, she was gorgeous with her dark hair spread out against the snowy comforter and her cheeks pink with excitement. And no bra under that sweater.

He backed off.

"Giving up?"

"Repositioning." Spanning her waist with both hands, he scooted her farther up on the mattress. Bonus, her unfastened jeans came partway off, taking her panties along for the ride. "That'll do." He grabbed hold of them. "Definitely wet."

"Told you." She was breathing fast, which made that soft sweater tremble.

"I believe you also wanted me to notice these." He drew her sweater up and tucked it under her chin.

"Possibly."

"Message received." He settled in, taking one pert nipple into his mouth as he slid his hand between her thighs.

She came quickly, which was what he'd intended. His cock desperately wanted to join the party but that wasn't gonna happen.

She needed to call Claudie. He needed to make sure they ate dinner. After that, they'd have uninterrupted time to explore the possibilities.

Mila was here, in his space, in his bed. She wanted him as much as he wanted her. He still couldn't quite believe his good fortune. But he'd fudging make the most of it.

<u>6</u>

Giddy from the prospect of more sexual adventures with Cole, Mila did a lousy job of sounding casual on the phone with her sister. Claudie would grill her when she came home.

Whenever that was. The later she came through the door, the more Claudie would suspect something had happened.

"Sounded like she was giving you a hard time." Cole stood in front of the stove making grilled cheese sandwiches that smelled great. A saucepan of tomato soup sent up tendrils of steam.

"She was just being Claudie." She'd spent the phone conversation gazing at him and wishing every woman in the world could have a moment like this. First he'd loved the daylights out of her. Then he'd loaned her a pair of sweats and set about fixing her dinner. What more could a girl ask for?

He glanced over his shoulder. "Do you think she knows?"

"She strongly suspects. She's been teasing me about you ever since the wedding." She set his phone on the kitchen island. "What can I do to help?"

"Bowls and plates are in the cupboard to my right, placemats and napkins in the left-hand drawer under the island. Utensils in the drawer next to it."

"*Bien.*" She left the plates and bowls on the counter by the stove and moved over to the kitchen island. Two stools faced the fireplace. "I'd better move this Christmas tree. Where should it go?"

"Anywhere's fine."

"I'll set it on an end table for now, but it needs to be near a socket so you can plug in the lights."

"Understood."

She wanted to see how it looked in his space when it was lit, but now wasn't the time to fool with that. "The Beaver Bunch only got to do one song. Would they like to give us a show during dinner?"

"Probably. I'll ask them."

"Do they have names?" She'd found napkin rings and pulled the napkins through them.

"Sure do. The fiddle player's Rufus, the one on the washboard is Buster and that's Shorty on the washtub bass."

"Great names."

"I didn't make them up. Those were our stage names when I was with the jug band."

She turned around, delighted with that tidbit of info. "You were Rufus?"

"Yes, ma'am." He flipped the sandwiches. "What do you want to drink?"

"Whatcha got, Rufus?"

He chuckled. "Water and beer. And coffee or tea if you want something hot."

"I just had something hot. I need something to cool me down."

"How you talk." Sliding the sandwiches on the plates, he carried them over to the island.

"It's your fault. Now I have orgasm brain."

"Join the club." His gaze swept over her. "There's nothing sexy about my baggy sweats until you put them on. Then when you move, that soft material manages to perfectly define your—"

"Something's burning."

"Fudge!" Whirling around, he grabbed the soup pan. "Damn it." He sighed. "How do you feel about blackened tomato soup?"

"Just pour it into the bowls and add a little sugar."

"Sugar?"

"Trust me, it works." She spied the sugar canister on the counter. "I'll do it."

"And I'll watch and learn." He divided the soup between the two bowls and ran water in the scorched pan. It hissed and threw up a cloud of steam. "Good thing it didn't boil over."

"Yeah, this is nothing. A tiny glitch." Picking up a soup spoon, she crossed to the counter and grabbed a teaspoon out of the silverware drawer. "You just add a tiny bit of sugar and then taste-test. If it's not right, you add a little more."

"Sounds like you've burned soup before."

"Doesn't everybody? Mom taught me this ages ago." She added a quarter teaspoon to each bowl and stirred. "Now we taste."

"If it's no good, I have more soup."

"And throw this away? No, no, no. We don't waste food around here." She dipped the soup spoon into one of the bowls, blew on it and then put it in her mouth. "Mm." She swallowed. "Needs a little more. Do you have any parmesan? That helps, too." She added a pinch of sugar to each bowl and stirred it in.

"And here I thought this meal would be quick and easy." He took a can of grated parmesan out of the fridge and set it on the counter.

"*No importa.*" She glanced at him. "I like a challenge."

"Lucky me."

She could get used to those warm looks and cute half-smiles. Dipping up more soup, she offered it to him. "See what you think."

He held her gaze as she fed him the soup. She hadn't meant it to be an erotic moment, but suddenly she wanted to kiss him more than she wanted to breathe.

Slowly she pulled the spoon away, her heart pounding. "Well?"

"Delicious." He grabbed her, his lips hot and demanding as he captured her mouth.

The soup spoon clattered to the floor as she climbed him like a tree, hooking her legs around his hips.

Cupping her tush, he carried her back through the barn doors, tumbled her onto the bed and followed her down. Panting with eagerness, he pulled off her clothes and his. His chest heaved as he knelt between her thighs and rolled on a condom.

Then he was there, thrusting fast, lifting her off the mattress. "Come for me."

His husky command sent her over the edge. Crying out, she arched into him. The rolling waves of her climax swept away her inhibitions and unleashed a string of her favorite Spanish swear words.

With a bellow of triumph, he drove home one more time. The pulse of his climax blended with the sweet aftershocks of hers. She held on tight, absorbing the shudders of his body, basking in the heat of his gaze.

As his breathing slowed, a smile tilted the corners of his mouth. "Extensive vocabulary, lady."

"Ah, but you don't know what I said."

"Ah, but I do. I work construction."

Her cheeks heated. "Oh."

"I liked it." He leaned down and kissed her hot cheeks. "Sounded like you were having fun."

"So much fun."

"Dinner will be cold." He kissed the tip of her nose. "I don't have a microwave."

"We'll pretend the soup's gazpacho."

"That's funny. What about the sandwiches?"

"We'll cut them into strips for dipping in the gazpacho. I'd also like to add that parmesan before we eat the soup."

"Then I'll meet you in the kitchen." Easing away, he left the bed.

Watching him go would never get old. She allowed herself to ogle, but once he was out of sight she located her sweater and the sweats he'd loaned her. Because they had cuffs and a drawstring, she'd made them work.

She couldn't imagine why he found them sexy, though. Then again, she enjoyed looking at him in sweats, especially because she knew what was underneath.

Dressing took no time whatsoever. Walking barefoot into the kitchen, she washed her hands, opened the parmesan and sprinkled some in each bowl. Then she sliced the sandwiches into finger-sized strips. As she carried everything over to the island, he came through the barn doors and walked toward her.

Her pulse hammered and her breath caught. They'd just had an explosive episode and yet her body didn't think that was enough. One glance at his manly self and the insistent ache began all over again.

"You probably shouldn't look at me like that or we won't ever have this dinner." His words were teasing but the gleam in his eyes said he wasn't. A word from her and they'd be back in his bedroom.

She gulped. "I don't know what's wrong with me. I've never been like this."

"Neither have I." He braced his hands on the other side of the island, as if deliberately keeping the structure between them. "It's wonderful... and scary."

"Maybe it's because we kept the lid on for so many months."

"Maybe." Emotion flickered in his eyes. Then he pushed away from the island. "We didn't settle on drinks."

"*Cerveza, por favor.*"

"That works for me, too. Have a seat. I'll get us a couple of bottles." He rounded the island and headed for the fridge. "Want a glass?"

"Don't need one. But thanks for asking." She slid onto a stool, her back to him, all her senses tuned to the clink of the bottles, the thump of the refrigerator door, the whisper of his bare feet on the wood floor, the sound of his breathing.

"I didn't really need to ask." He took the stool next to her, twisted off the cap on the beer and handed it over. "I knew the answer. You like drinking from the bottle."

"So do you. And your limit is two."

He smiled. "And your limit is flexible." He twisted the cap off his bottle and took a sip.

"Hey, my brother was getting married. If you can't get tipsy on your brother's wedding day, when can you?"

"And if Jordie and Luis hadn't fallen in love...."

"We'd never have met."

His gaze was steady. "Tough to imagine."

"Just now you said this is wonderful *and* scary. You're scared?"

"Yep. You?"

"Uh-huh." She took a breath. "You're out of my comfort zone, Cole Sterling."

"Backatcha."

"But...I want to see where this takes us."

"Me, too."

"To Luis and Jordan." She lifted her bottle in his direction.

He tapped it with his. "To leaving comfort zones."

7

Cole wasn't used to getting what he asked for. This setup was exactly what he'd envisioned back in June when he'd left his unsatisfying job and ended a tepid relationship.

Mila was the woman he'd always wanted — imaginative, principled, funny, sexy. He'd felt a zing of recognition from the moment they'd met. Being in charge of ranch maintenance suited him to a T. No two days were the same and he couldn't ask for better folks to hang with.

On top of that, he got to see his sister on a regular basis. He'd missed her like crazy when she'd created a business that kept her on the road. But now she traveled less and when she was home, she was steps away.

Hell yeah, he was scared it might all disappear. And excited for the chance he'd been given to finally get it right.

"Did you ask the Beaver Bunch if they'd play for us?"

"I forgot." He flashed her a grin. "Had other things on my mind." Putting down his beer, he slipped off the stool and headed over to those critters. She hadn't seen everything they could do.

The control box door was still open, the main switch still on. Once he'd kissed her, those animatronic critters had taken a back seat. He picked up a wireless mic he had hanging on the wall and turned it on.

He didn't need a mic since Mila could hear him just fine, but he might as well practice using it. "Hey, Rufus! We'd be much obliged if you boys would play us a tune." Then he hit one of the many switches in front of him.

Rufus turned his head in Cole's direction and his mouth moved. "On it, boss! Whatcha hankerin' fer?"

Mila whooped in delight. "That's you?"

"Heck, no. That's Rufus. That's how he talks."

She giggled. "Love it."

He glanced back at the trio. "How about *On the Road Again*?"

"Copy that, boss!" Rufus turned toward the others as Cole punched in the selection. He didn't have many numbers loaded yet, but eventually he'd have a couple of hours worth.

Cuing up a jug band version of Willie Nelson's classic, he added two more tunes, a jug band rendition of Johnny Cash's *Ring of Fire* and *Do You Believe in Magic* by the Lovin' Spoonful. All three came from a flash drive of recordings made by his old jug band. Good thing he'd saved it.

Closing the control box door, he returned to Mila as those beavers launched into their routine. She was an appreciative audience, giving them all her attention as she ate her sandwich and soup.

He pretended to be watching them, too, but instead he focused all his senses on her. He still couldn't quite believe his good fortune.

He'd already thanked Jordie for inviting him out to the ranch on that fateful July Fourth, but it had been a generalized statement of gratitude. Someday soon he'd thank her specifically for the life-changing opportunity to share space with Mila.

They'd almost finished their simple dinner by the time the music ended. Mila put down her beer and applauded the trio. "Well done Rufus, Buster and Shorty!" She turned to him. "They're fantastic, Cole. I love that Rufus talks. The raccoons don't do that."

"They might, soon. Clem said he felt an update coming on, probably after the first of the year."

"You inspired him."

"We inspire each other. It never occurred to me I'd run into another animatronics nerd."

"He's probably thinking the same. But he doesn't have time to fool with them during the Christmas season. Speaking of that, have you thought about giving the Beaver Bunch Santa hats like the raccoons have?"

A flicker of unease invaded the happy glow he had going on. "I didn't. Probably too late to order any."

"True, but I'll bet we could still find regular ones in town. I'm pretty good with a needle. I could modify them for you."

Mild panic set in. "I'd hate to put you to the trouble. You must be busy doing—"

"Not really. All my family gifts are ready to go. Claudie and I mailed off the Christmas cards to the Hearts & Hooves supporters last week. Our holiday adoption push winds up tomorrow. How soon would you like to unveil these guys?"

"It can be anytime, now that you've seen them. How about this weekend?" He needed to get it done before the twenty-third, when he was scheduled to get sick.

"Part of me wants to do that, but you've kept the secret this long. Wouldn't it be more spectacular if it was part of the celebration, like on Christmas Eve?"

He managed to control a shudder. "Well, I—"

"No, that might be too dicey, weather-wise, but if Christmas Day is sunny, you could do it then. So far they're predicting decent weather on Christmas. We might get snow before then, but then it'll clear off."

He started to sweat. This is what he got for being so focused on completing the project so he could show it to Mila. Even without that single-mindedness, he might not have realized the holiday was coming up. He'd spent fifteen years ignoring it. "Don't you—" Pausing, he cleared his throat. "Don't you have plenty of other things going on that day?"

"We deliberately *don't* have a lot going on. We just hang out with each other, eating and playing whatever game Mom gets for the family. If the conditions are good for the sleigh, we hitch up Woody and Buzz and take turns going for a ride."

"There's a sleigh somewhere?"

"That's what's under the tarp in the tractor barn."

"Huh. I never looked."

"We haven't taken it out yet because you need at least six inches of packed snow and lately it keeps turning to slush. If we get fresh snow, we build forts, make snow people, have snowball fights. In other words, it would be a perfect day for introducing the Beaver Bunch."

As he gazed into those beautiful eyes, the excitement and anticipation shining there made his chest hurt. What now?

He could tell her how he felt about Christmas and watch her happiness turn to sadness and concern. He could agree to the plan knowing he'd sabotage it in the end. Or he could white-knuckle it though Christmas Day.

There really was only one choice. At least she hadn't set her heart on Christmas Eve. He'd find a way out of celebrating that with the family. Food poisoning was an option.

He sucked in a breath. "Then let's bring those critters out on the big day."

"Awesome! Do you want me to make the Santa hats? I'd love to."

Might as well go all in. "That would be great."

"It also gives me an excuse to be here. I can tell everyone I've seen your secret project and we decided to add a festive element to it. I'll modify them here instead of at home."

"Good plan." He might not like the hat idea, but if she'd work on them here, he'd learn to like it.

She laughed. "I thought you'd approve. Could we pick them up together sometime tomorrow? What's your schedule like?"

"Your mom asked me to look at the hinges on the main gate in the morning. If I end up replacing them, it could take me a while, but so far my afternoon's free."

"If it stays that way, we could go then."

"Okay." Driving into town with her would be fun. Looking at Santa hats, which would probably be smack dab in the middle of a bunch of holiday decorations, not so much.

She peered at him. "Is that a problem? You look a little stressed."

He launched into the first silly excuse he could find. "Me and the boys just realized it's almost showtime and we have stage fright."

"Aww." She gave him a warm smile. "My family will go crazy over those little guys. You know they will."

"I didn't know it for sure. That's why I invited you for a preview. I figured if you liked these critters, there was a good chance the rest of the family would."

"Really? You had doubts about that?"

"Sure. I've only lived here for six months."

"I keep forgetting that. It feels longer to me. You fit in so well. You and Jordan both do. I'll bet she's seen this already."

"No, ma'am."

"No? But you two are so close!"

"That's the point. She's gonna rave about anything I've made. I could throw something together with a few sticks and baling wire and she'd call it a masterpiece. I needed an unbiased opinion."

She met his gaze. "Then you should have asked Claudie. You had to know I'm not unbiased."

He flushed. "Okay, I wanted to impress you."

"Mission accomplished. But since I'm not unbiased, how can you trust what I—"

"Because you're not my sister."

"Thank goodness for that!"

"Stay with me. She hasn't lived here long enough to know for sure what would appeal to your family. You have. Also, if you thought they wouldn't like the Beaver Bunch for some reason you'd tell me. You'd want to save me from being embarrassed."

"I would. But I promise they'll be nuts about your creation. Blown away. I can't wait for Christmas Day when they get to see it."

"The weather could change." He could always hope.

"If it does would you be okay with bringing everyone up here?"

Whoops. Weather wouldn't save him, after all. "Sure."

"Good, because it might come to that if a storm—"

His phone rang. Happy to interrupt their troubling conversation, he excused himself and went to grab it from the kitchen counter. "It's your mom."

"Don't tell her I'm—no, wait, you need to tell her I'm here. Just don't say—"

"You think I would?"

"No, no—just answer it! The longer it rings—"

"Right." He tapped the speaker mode so Mila could hear the conversation. "Hi, Raquel."

"I'm so sorry to interrupt your evening, *amigo,* but that pipe under the sink you warned me about chose to start leaking ten minutes ago. I've turned off the main valve but Greta and I are in the middle of a complicated baking session. Could you—"

"I'll be right there. I picked up a PVC pipe a couple months ago knowing I'd eventually need it."

"Bless you. *Lo siento.*"

"No worries. I was just—"

"Gotta go. Greta needs me. 'Bye." She disconnected.

"You didn't tell her."

"She didn't give me a chance. I'll mention it while I'm there."

"How long will it take?"

"At least a couple of hours."

She picked up her dishes and carried them to the sink. "Then I think I'd better get dressed and go home."

"Afraid so. Sorry."

She smiled. "Not your fault. If it's okay with you, I'll let Claudie know this addition to the secret project will take hours."

"Will it?"

"Heck, no."

"Excellent." He hesitated. "How do you want to play this with your family?"

"You mean about us?"

"Yes, ma'am."

"I'll have to tell Claudie. She can read me too well. But she'll keep it to herself if I ask her."

"What do you want to do?"

"I'd rather not broadcast it, yet. It'll come out soon enough, but let's just enjoy the privacy while we can."

"Works for me." Pulling her close, he gave her a gentle kiss. "*Manana.*"

"*Manana, mi cielo.*"

His Spanish was limited mostly to swear words, but he was pretty sure that *mi cielo* meant *my heaven.* And how he loved hearing those words coming from Mila's sweet lips. All things considered, one day of hell wasn't such a high price to pay, after all.

8

Composing herself as best she could, Mila took off her coat and snow boots in the foyer. Breathing pine-scented air mingled with the aroma of cedar smoke helped. The combination of six trees of various sizes and a woodburning fireplace made the house smell delicious.

"You're taking forever to come in," Claudie called out from the living room. "Is there a problem?"

"No." Mila took one more deep breath. "Just enjoying how nice the house smells." She walked into the cozy living room she shared with her sister.

Claudie's crochet needle flashed in the glow from the beehive fireplace as she worked on a Christmas tree skirt. She'd pulled her thick brown hair into a ponytail because she insisted it helped her concentrate when her hair was away from her face.

She glanced up. "Well?"

Mila couldn't seem to do anything but stand there and grin. There were no words.

Her sister leaped up and laid aside her needlework. "You two did it!"

"We did."

"Oh, my God! Finally!" Racing toward her, Claudie gave her a tight hug. "I knew it." She stepped back, beaming. "I just knew he wasn't asking you up there just to look at his special project. Was it good?"

"What do you think?"

Her sister laughed. "I only asked because it's fun to see you get red. How many times?"

"Hey, I'm not gonna—"

"C'mon. Let me live vicariously."

"Twice, and we would've— well, Mom called with a plumbing emergency, so—"

"She *didn't*! Well, fudge, as Cole would say. That sucks. Why didn't you stay and wait for hm?"

"The pipe under the sink finally broke. He said it could take a couple of hours at least."

"Stupid pipe. Rotten timing. Dad was supposed to fix the damn thing, and then...."

"I think that's why she put off having Cole replace it."

"Oh, definitely. Whenever he does a repair Dad would've done, she feels it. You can tell."

"She's not the only one. I think about it, too."

"So do I. We probably all do. But I'm so glad we hired Cole." She chuckled. "I'll bet you're *really* glad."

"You could say that."

"So what's the status? I assume you'll continue what you started."

"Yes."

"You just lit up like a Christmas tree when you said that."

"That's what I feel like. As if someone turned on a switch inside me."

Claudie laughed. "Someone did, and his name is Cole Sterling. Are you telling everyone?"

"Just you for now, *hermana*."

She nodded. "I get that, but they'll guess something's going on. You look *really* happy."

"Of course I do. It's Christmas."

"And you just got an early present. Will you be sneaking over there for fun and games?"

"Sort of, but at this point I have a cover story. I'm making a small addition to his secret project and I'll work on it at his place to keep from giving anything away."

"Clever. And what is this secret project? I'm all ears."

"I'm not going to tell you."

"Mila!"

"You need to see it for yourself, when everyone else does. Even if I tried to describe it, I couldn't do it justice."

"Well, damn. Can you give me a hint?"

"I'll just say this. Dad would have loved it."

"Oh, wow. Now I can't wait. How soon before he trots it out?"

"Christmas Day."

"You're killing me, here. I thought for sure you'd come back with a vivid description. I'm already keeping one secret. Why not go for two?"

"Describing it is not the same as seeing it in action."

"Aha! It moves!"

"Forget I said that."

"It moves, Dad would love it, and Cole's unveiling it on Christmas Day. Please tell me it's not a Santa robot. That would be creepy."

"Dad would hate a Santa robot."

"You're right, he would. Hmm. I suppose it could be a fancy new gate. Gates move and Dad loved his gates, but I can't imagine what you'd be making to enhance it. Maybe hang a wreath on it. Am I getting close?"

"No."

"Good, because a fancy gate is a bad idea. We don't need more gates and we're not replacing any Dad put up, that's for sure. Is it like those reindeer that move and light up, the kind you put in the yard?"

"No and stop guessing. You'll never guess it anyway. Not in a million years."

"You're actually not going to tell me? You said you would."

"I did not."

"Yes, you did. When I asked what you thought he'd created, you said *we'll see.* So who's the *we* in that? You and me, that's who."

"It's just an expression. Honest, Claud, you don't want me to tell you. It will ruin the moment when you get to see if for real."

"O-*kay.*" She let out a groan. "If you're not going to spill the beans on his secret project, you at least have to tell what it was like knocking boots with him. Come sit." Claudie grabbed her hand and tugged.

She planted her feet. "I'm not gonna."

"Pretty please. I've been living like a nun for months, and I—"

"Your choice."

"Exactly. Inspire me. Tell me it was amazing, life-changing, made you feel like a woman."

"I felt like a woman before I went up there."

"Because you had the hots for him, that's why. I haven't had the hots for a man in so long I've forgotten what it's like."

"You were giving Cole the eye when he first arrived. I thought maybe we'd end up fighting over him."

"So did I. There's lots to like about that cowboy. I figured I could work up some enthusiasm. Then I saw the sparks fly between you two and realized I was just trying to talk myself into flirting with him."

"Your guy's out there. He just hasn't shown up yet."

"If you say so. Is Cole your guy?"

The question startled her. "It's too soon to tell." The cautious answer popped out of her mouth like candy from a vending machine. *We're cautious people.*

But her automatic response hadn't been truthful. She'd known from the day she'd first laid eyes on Cole Sterling that he was her guy. If Claudie had wanted him, they would have been in for one helluva fight.

9

Although Cole would rather have spent the past few hours making love to Mila, working under the sink in Raquel's kitchen had its rewards. The scent of chocolate cake wafted from the oven. He'd even been allowed to taste the chocolate mousse that became the filling for each of the three Yule logs Raquel and Greta were making.

He wouldn't get to sample the finished product, since the cakes would be tucked away in the spare refrigerator in the pantry until Christmas Eve. He wouldn't be around then and he doubted there would be leftovers on Christmas Day.

His walk from the barn to the house had been instructive, too. He hadn't strolled around the area after dark recently. Instead he'd stayed closeted in his loft working on the Beaver Bunch with the blinds pulled down for both privacy and warmth.

Turned out Laughing Creek Ranch became a fairyland at Christmas, with lights twinkling from every house and even some of the evergreens. It was so removed from his own experience that he didn't react to the display with the same nausea that plagued him when he entered stores this time of year and heard Christmas carols on the sound system.

The ranch house might have affected him that way except he'd headed straight for the kitchen where he'd been inundated with the aroma of chocolate cakes in the oven. His mother didn't bake at Christmas or any other time, really.

Since Raquel and Greta couldn't give him any of the cake when he'd finished installing the pipe, they insisted on feeding him cookies and hot chocolate. After he joined them at the table, he checked the clock on the wall. Midnight. Too late to contact Mila.

He glanced at them as they sipped from their own whipped-cream-topped mugs. "Do you normally stay up this late?"

Raquel smiled. "Did you think after we pulled you away from your warm loft and kept you up late that we'd leave you alone to finish the job and let yourself out?"

"That would have been fine."

Greta lifted her chin. "We don't operate that way, do we, Mom?"

"No, *mija*, we don't." She looked across the table at him. "For all I know you were in the midst of working on your secret project. I've seen your light on late into the night."

"Actually, the project's done."

"It is?" Greta practically bounced in her chair. "When can we see it?"

Raquel laughed. "Someone's been dying of curiosity."

"Yeah, like you haven't, Mom. We all have. For two months we've all been staring up at the loft wondering about this mysterious thing you're creating. The suspense is *killing* us."

"Wow. Didn't mean to bring the drama."

"Aw, sure you did." Greta gave him a playful punch on the arm. "I'm just teasing you. It's been fun. So when's the big reveal?"

"I discussed that with Mila tonight."

"Has *she* seen it? I thought for sure Jordan would have, but she said—"

"Let him talk, *mija*." Raquel regarded him with a steady gaze.

Her eyes were so like Mila's, only with a few crinkles at the corners. He shifted in his chair. After six months of living here, he recognized that look.

Both women had it. It meant they were processing. Raquel was likely going over what he'd said and drawing some conclusions about his decision to show Mila first.

He had some tricky territory to navigate. "I asked her to take a look and make sure it's something that you all will like."

"What did she—" Greta glanced at her mother, then looked over at him and sighed. "Sorry. Keep going, please."

He gave her a smile. She reminded him of Jordie at twenty-two. Same blonde hair, same irrepressible energy. "She loved it."

"Awesome!"

"She thinks Christmas Day would be the perfect time to unveil it."

Greta made a face. "That's almost a week away!"

He hadn't counted on pushback. Could he get a reprieve? "It's not set in stone. If your mom thinks another time would be better, I'm open to suggestions."

"Christmas Day sounds good to me. It's a gift from you to the family, right?"

"Yes, ma'am." He could agree with a clear conscience because she hadn't labeled it a Christmas gift.

"And we'll all be hanging around that day, whereas between now and then we'll have plenty of stuff going on. Which reminds me, are you going into town with us tomorrow night? We'll be carpooling."

"What's happening tomorrow night?"

"You forgot the Christmas party at the Raccoon!" Greta gaped at him. "You really have been focused on that project. But now it's done, so yay, you can go."

"I guess I can." He did his best to sound happy about it. He couldn't very well pretend to be sick tomorrow night and then be sick again on Christmas Eve.

"Of course you'll take your fiddle." Greta's blue eyes gleamed with eagerness. "I'm sure you know some Christmas carols."

"Funny thing about that. I don't."

"No problem. Mila can hum them for you."

She certainly could but that didn't mean he should risk having a reaction to those tunes. On the other hand, he'd loved teaming up with her back in October. Sitting in with the Rooty Toots had been a blast, too.

"Greta and I will be taking the ranch van and we'd have room for you if you'd like to ride with us."

"Thanks for the offer, but since I'm not much of a drinker, maybe I should take my truck and be another designated driver."

Raquel nodded. "That's a great offer. I'll pass the word and I'm sure you'll have some takers. We'll leave around five."

"Sounds good." He finished his hot chocolate and gave the clock another glance. "Thanks for the treats. I'd better take off and let you two get some sleep. Can't have you dozing off in the middle of the party."

Raquel chuckled. "I'm planning to take a nap tomorrow afternoon. Historically the Bridger Bunch is the life of the party."

"Especially my grandma and the aunties," Greta said. "If you thought they were something at the wedding, wait until you see them rock out at this Christmas party. They look forward to it all year."

"Should be fun." Truer words were never said. It should be and probably would be for everyone else. He'd be praying he could make it through in one piece.

<u>10</u>

Mila was up long before Claudie the next morning. Technically they were both on Christmas break and didn't need to respond to emails or check the Hearts & Hooves adoption site on a regular basis.

But she carried her coffee, apple, peanut butter toast and phone into the office anyway. After plugging in the lights on the five-foot Douglas fir in the corner and cueing up some Mannheim Steamroller on her phone, she brought up the website to tackle an update she'd been putting off.

Instead she found herself clicking on a recently created menu item, *Behind the Scenes*, featuring images of Laughing Creek's new maintenance chief. She clicked through them slowly, savoring each one, enlarging them to study the detail.

One showed Cole carrying a couple of planks on one broad shoulder, a toolbelt riding on his slim hips. In another he was smoothing out a newly poured slab of cement on a blistering hot day. Sweat molded his white T-shirt to his chest as he labored, his Stetson pulled low over his eyes.

In a more recent shot he was in profile kneeling on the roof of the main house, the snow-covered Flint Creek Range in the background. He'd turned up the collar of his jacket to block the November wind as he nailed down some loose shingles.

She zoomed in to study the slope of his nose, the squint lines at the corner of his eye, the set of his strong jaw covered with his trademark bristle. So soft against her skin. Her body clenched with longing.

She'd saved her favorite for last — Cole on Sparky, the rehabilitated chestnut Luis had given him in late September, checking the fence line. Enlarging the shot made it pixelate a little, but she could still make out his happy smile.

From the moment Luis and Rio had started training that horse, Cole had shown an interest in the big gelding. He'd found excuses to hang around while her brothers had gradually turned the chestnut from a wild creature into a well-mannered companion.

Luis had waited for Cole to indicate he'd like to have the horse. When he'd finally inquired about the price, Luis had only asked for a handshake.

According to Luis, it had been the most energetic handshake in history. And the most silent. Cole had been struck speechless by the gift.

When *Deck the Halls* was interrupted with the ping of a text, she had a hunch who'd sent it. Her heart rate picked up. Sure enough.

Good morning. Looks like I'll be one of the designated drivers tonight. Want to ride in with me?

You know I do. I'd totally forgotten that party.

He responded with a smiling emoji wearing a cowboy hat, followed by another message. *I'll text you when I'm almost finished with the gate hinge. If it's not too late, we could grab lunch in town.*

Love to. Will you be working alone out there?

Why do you ask?

I might take Sol for a ride. I could come check on you.

I'd love the company.

Then I will. See you then.

Can't wait.

The simple exchange made her shiver with eagerness. Pictures were nice, but she'd rather interact with the real thing.

"Aha!"

Mila jumped and turned in her chair. "No fair sneaking up on me!"

"How else could I confirm that you're in here mooning over that cowboy? I was feeling guilty thinking you were working and then I saw him." Claudie pointed toward the screen. "You're welcome, by the way. Adding that section to the website was my idea." She took a sip from the mug in her hand. "I took the pictures, too."

"That's what made me worry that you liked him. Great pictures."

"He's a good subject. Very masculine. Not your pretty-boy type. I appreciate him aesthetically, but he doesn't get my panties wet."

"Well, I'm grateful. I would've hated to have to fight you for him."

Her sister laughed. "I'll bet you would have hated it. We've established I'm a better fighter."

"The hairclip fight? That must have been—geez, seventeen years ago."

"See? It stuck in your mind, too. That was our last real fight and I won. I have the hairclip to prove it."

"Still? I never see you wear it."

"My tastes have changed since then."

"If you don't like it anymore, why keep it?"

"Because I fought hard for it."

"I remember. I ended up with a bloody nose. That's when I gave up." She gazed at her beautiful, fierce, creative and sentimental sister.

Claudie had on her usual winter morning outfit, flannel pjs and the bathrobe their dad had given her at least ten Christmases ago. It was permanently stained from various projects and one end of the sash was charred from the time she'd caught it on fire. Nobody dared suggest she get rid of it.

She waved at the screen, which had now gone dark. "I assume you'll be going with him to the party tonight."

"I am. In fact, he just texted that he's volunteered to be a designated driver, so if you want to ride with us, you'd better text him and say so before his back seat fills up with our brothers."

"Abso-fudging-lutely." She pulled her phone out of her pocket and tapped rapidly on the screen. "I'm dying to see how you guys navigate this gathering."

"To be honest, I'd forgotten about it until he texted me just now."

"You forgot the Raccoon Christmas party?" She looked up from her phone. "Girl, you never forget a major holiday event!"

"Yeah, I know. Surprised me, too. We cooked up this plan so I could legitimately be at his place while I made the additional item I'm adding to his secret project. I thought I'd be working on that tonight."

"Or not. Why work when you could be doing the horizontal Electric Slide?"

She flushed. "It's not a total smokescreen. I will be making something."

"It's called whoopie, sis. But I'm afraid you'll be getting a late start. That party always runs well after midnight."

"I know." She let out a sigh. "And I look forward to it all year. Normally I'd be excited, but after last night—"

"I get it. Brand-new boinking is more compelling than a party with your nearest and dearest. On the bright side, he'll probably bring his fiddle. That'll be a treat."

"For him, too. He used to play in a band, so sitting in with the Rooty Toots is fun for him. I need to remember that."

"Don't worry. He's likely as impatient with this party routine as you are. I can't remember if you danced with him at the wedding or not. I can't picture you two out on the floor, so I think not."

"Only line dances. Mostly we were on the bandstand."

"I predict that will change tonight. Just remember to keep it PG."

"Claudie, for Pete's sake. Have you ever known me to do otherwise?"

She grinned. "No, but I've never known you to forget the Christmas party. We're in unchartered territory, *hermana*."

11

The rhythmic thud of hoofbeats carried far in the cold stillness of a Montana morning. Cole laid his tools on the tailgate of his truck and stripped off his gloves. Mila could still be a couple of minutes away, but he'd get a kiss out of this visit or know the reason why.

He didn't want to touch her with cold hands, though, so he shoved them in his jacket pockets and scanned the area. The road, crisscrossed with tire tracks embedded in a thick crust of ice, was empty.

A flash of gold in a thick stand of evergreens told him she'd chosen a trail instead of the road. Stepping through the open gate, he went to meet her.

The narrow path to his left was faint, likely used by wild horses more often than Laughing Creek riders. Mila would know those trails well. Coming this way instead of using the road told him she hadn't wanted to advertise her morning ride.

Even more telling, she'd worn a suede sheepskin jacket instead of her red parka. She couldn't do much about her flashy horse, though.

All the more reason for him to meet her in the cover of the trees.

He lost track of her after he'd trudged several yards into the forest. Ah. There she was, ducking under the branch of a tall ponderosa as she rode toward him.

She straightened and pulled Sol to a halt. "You came to meet me."

He kept walking, pushing his hands deep into his pockets. "Figured I stood a better chance of kissing you if we weren't standing in the middle of the road."

Her gaze traveled in that direction. "I can't even see your truck from this spot."

"Kinda the point." When he got to her, he took hold of the palomino's bridle and stroked his velvet neck. "Hey, Sol. How're you doing, buddy?"

"Where are your gloves?"

He glanced up and tilted his hat back. "Left them on the tailgate. Care to come down from there? Or do you want me to come up?"

Grinning, she looped the reins around the horn and dismounted. "Let's not confuse Sol."

"Let's not." Reaching for her, he pulled her close.

"Wait. I'll take off my gloves, too." She tucked them in her coat pocket and nestled against him. "Hi."

"Hi, yourself." One look into those deep brown eyes brought it all back — the taste of her mouth, the feel of her skin, the welcoming heat of her body when he—

"I thought you were going to kiss me."

"I am. I'm just...remembering."

"Me, too."

"We had a lot fewer layers."

She chuckled. "Mostly none."

"You know what? My hands are getting cold."

"You could put them inside my coat."

"What a concept." Heart thumping, he began unfastening the buttons. "How about you? Are your hands cold?"

"Freezing." She unzipped his jacket and slid her arms inside. "That's better."

"Way better." He followed suit, pulling her in tight with a sigh as her warm, tempting body sent his into overdrive. "God, you feel good."

She moaned softly. "You, too. I thought we'd have tonight to ourselves."

"We could have early tomorrow morning to ourselves."

"I might fall asleep on you."

Lowering his head, he dipped under the brim of her hat. "Not if I can help it." He settled into a kiss that instantly short-circuited his brain.

He couldn't get enough of her lush mouth. She kissed the way she made love, holding nothing back. He lost track of everything but the urge to stoke the fire, letting it rage out of control until they surrendered their bodies to the flames.

Her soft whimper sent a message to his lust-fogged brain. He had to touch her, had to at least—

A horn beeped. He stilled. And registered that he'd unfastened her jeans. His hand was halfway to its destination.

She broke away from the kiss. "Someone's... someone's—"

"At the gate." He barely got the words past his clogged throat. Slowly he withdrew his hand from her jeans.

She gulped for air. "You'd better go see."

"Stay here."

"Okay."

Backing away from her, he zipped his coat. "Be right there!" he called out as he glanced down at his fly. Oh, boy. Couldn't go out like that.

He turned his back. "Don't watch this," he murmured.

Unzipping, he freed his cock, scooped up a little snow lying in a shady spot on the forest floor, clenched his teeth and sprinkled it over the evidence. After a quick swipe with his bandana, he zipped up and faced Mila again.

She was quietly having hysterics, tears of laughter rolling down her cheeks. Tugging down the brim of his hat, he touched two fingers to the brim and left, lengthening his stride as he retraced his steps to the gate.

Rio's red truck sat on the right side of the road by the open gate. When Cole appeared, Rio lowered his window. "Figured you were answering nature's call, but I decided to beep anyway, just to let you know I was out here. Hope I didn't rush you."

"No worries." Cole crossed to the truck. "What's up?"

"I had to run into town for some last-minute Christmas shopping and didn't see Mom's text about your offer to drive tonight until I stopped for gas. Do you still have room for me in your truck?"

"Probably." He took out his phone and checked for texts. "Looks like it. Claudie asked me this morning and here's a request from Monty. That's all so far, so you're in. Now I'm full up."

"Your truck seats five, right? That's only four. I wonder if Zay—"

"I forgot to say I'm taking Mila."

"Oh. That's cool. Can I have the front seat? Monty likes the back and my sisters probably want to sit together."

"Sorry, dude. Mila gets the front."

Rio did a double-take. Then a slow smile lit up his movie-star handsome face. "I see."

Cole didn't respond, just kept his gaze steady.

"Well, then. I'll be seeing you tonight at five. Thanks for volunteering to be the DD."

"You're welcome."

As Rio started rolling up his window, a loud whinny drifted from the forest. Pausing with the window halfway up, he glanced at Cole. "Interesting."

"Probably a mustang."

"Maybe." Amusement sparkled in his eyes. "Sure sounded like Sol, though. That horse really likes me. Calls out like that when he hears my voice."

Cole shrugged. "I guess Mila could be taking a ride this morning."

"Guess so. See you tonight." Flashing him a big smile, he rolled up the window and drove through the gate.

Dragging in a breath of cold air, Cole made his way back to Mila. "Did you get any of that?"

"Clear as a bell. He knows." She'd buttoned her coat and likely zipped her jeans, too. "That's on me. I was taking a risk coming out here, but I wanted to see you."

"I wanted to see you, too. As I'm sure you could tell."

"Claudie can keep a secret but Rio won't. This is too good a story and he won't be able to resist."

"I don't care. Do you?"

"Not really. The word would've gotten out sooner or later. Now that the party's replaced our private evening together, we might as well go public. Then nobody will be surprised if I end the night at your place."

"I like the sound of that." He kept his hands in his pockets. "I want to kiss you again, but—"

"Better not."

He sucked in another breath. "I only meant to kiss you."

"As I recall, that's all you meant to do the first time."

"Evidently I can't just kiss you without pushing for more."

She smiled. "I like that about you."

"You don't think I'm some uncontrolled maniac?"

"Oh, I do."

"And you're okay with it?"

"I'm very okay with it. That's what I've been looking for all my life."

He held her gaze and let those beautiful words sink in. "Me, too."

12

A little past noon, Mila climbed behind the wheel of her powder-blue truck and Cole swung up into the passenger seat.

"Nice truck."

"Thanks." Having his sexy self in the passenger seat gave her the fumbles and she had trouble getting the key in the ignition.

"You okay over there?"

"Just..." She managed to jab it in and start the motor. "Hyped up." His low chuckle turned her insides to molasses.

"So am I. Everything's... different."

"No kidding." She backed out of her parking spot next to the mini-hacienda. "I meant to invite you in to see the trees but I forgot."

"Another time."

"Want some Christmas music for the road?"

"How about if we just talk?"

"Fine with me. I don't need Christmas music. I'm already chock-a-block with the Christmas spirit. I have a feeling this will be one to remember."

"You could be right."

Taking a deep breath, she focused on driving instead of the extremely appealing man next to her. When he'd texted that he'd finished the gate repair and wanted to take her to lunch after they shopped, she'd offered to drive because she needed gas.

That was true, but she was also testing his willingness to be chauffeured by a woman. She'd happily let him pay for lunch since it was his idea, but this relationship had the makings of something serious, which put her on alert.

If he harbored any rigid beliefs about a woman's place, she wanted to know. He'd readily agreed to her plan and his relaxed posture told her he was fine riding shotgun. Great news.

Since he'd chosen conversation over holiday music, she started the ball rolling. "I was bummed about the party at first, but now I'm glad we're going. As you pointed out last night, we've never danced together."

"I've been thinking about that. It's almost as if we made a mutual decision. Did you ever consider asking me?"

"I did, but I hesitated. It felt like a big step."

"Same here. I wonder if we both sensed what might happen if we got that close."

From the corner of her eye she caught him watching her. "And we might start something we weren't ready for?"

"Exactly."

Her body began to tingle. Maybe music was a better choice. "Are we ready for it now?"

"God, I hope so. We'd better be, because there's no going back."

"Nope."

"I can't speak for you, but I needed these six months to settle in, get acclimated. Gather info."

"Info?"

"About you."

She laughed. "That's funny. Obviously I didn't need to settle in, but I've been gathering info about you, too."

"From Jordie, no doubt."

"I promise she was discreet. I don't think she told me anything you wouldn't want her to. It was all good stuff."

"Like I said, she has zero objectivity when it comes to me."

"Oh, I wouldn't say that."

"She talked trash about me?"

"Oh, no. She adores you." She paused behind the gate, which swung open without hesitation. "Nice job on the hinge."

"Thank you. So Jordie adores me, but what else did she say?"

"That you've always short-changed yourself." She drove through the gate and out to the highway. "She's hopeful you're on a new path."

"I am. Case in point. I'm here with you."

"That's flattering."

"It's not flattery. It's the truth. Six months ago I left a nice woman. Absolutely nothing wrong with her, except... now I know what I was missing."

She glanced at him. The heat in his gray eyes made her gulp. Heart pounding, she quickly brought her attention back to the road. "Now all I can think about is backseat sex."

"No can do. I didn't bring condoms. On purpose."

"Good, because everyone around here knows my truck." She took a shaky breath. "It's a bad idea. But I want to. I keep telling myself the newness is making me crazy. It'll wear off."

"Doesn't feel like it."

"Yeah, I know. Certainly not during this drive to town. Let's switch subjects. Who did you ask about me?"

"Everybody. I like to think I was subtle but I'll bet they all knew I had a crush."

"And what did you learn?"

"That they all look up to you as a leader. They think of Adam as a leader, too, but you're the one they tend to ask for advice. You're smart, steady, and have a Montana-sized heart."

"Aww."

"Claudie told me you two fought constantly growing up, but now you're best friends."

"We were desperate to stake out our territory. I know kids fight in families that aren't blended, but getting insta-siblings adds rocket fuel to those battles."

"You'd never know it now. This Bridger Bunch is solid."

"You might not have said so if you'd been here when Dad died, but we've got our feet under us, now. We're stronger than ever."

"Looks like it from where I stand." He hesitated. "I also know about your loser guy. But we don't have to talk about him if you don't want to."

"It's okay. I still can't believe I fell for his sob-story routine, but I totally bought it."

"Because you have a big heart."

"And a blind spot, it seems. When he mistreated me I gave him grace because he was damaged. Turns out he enjoyed being mean. Made him feel powerful."

"Sounds like a fudging bastard."

"Yep. Sometimes abused people end up becoming abusers."

"I suppose."

"He lived rent-free in my head way too long, first when I believed I could help him and later when I felt like a fool because he didn't want my help. He wanted control."

"I'm sorry."

"Here's the good news. I clearly booted him out of my head and made room for someone new, because here you are."

"Lucky me." He said if softly, almost reverently.

Happiness flooded through her, washing away the last vestiges of that terrible choice she'd made in the past. Not this time. "In case you can't tell, I'm grateful for you, Cole."

His breath hitched. "You can't imagine what that means to me. I won't let you down."

"I can't picture how you ever would. Hey, we're almost there. Which do you want to do first, shopping for the hats or lunch?"

"Shopping, please."

"Parking on the square will be a zoo, so I'll just take what I can find. We might have to walk a bit. Do you mind? My brothers aren't big on walking."

"Doesn't bother me."

"Glad to hear it." She braked at the stop sign and waited for traffic to clear before pulling onto the square. "Sing out if you see a space. I'd rather park here than in the overflow lot."

"You might have to, though. It's packed."

"It is, but oh, look! Someone's backing out of a spot in front of the barbershop. We're golden." She put on her turn signal and let out a sigh. "It's busy, but that's how it's supposed to be. I love coming to town during the countdown to Christmas."

"Yeah, it's very pretty."

"The Rockefeller Center tree in New York is gorgeous, but I'm partial to the one in our gazebo." She pulled into the parking spot and shut off the motor. "Not bad. Only half a block from the General Store."

"Let's do it." He unbuckled his seat belt and climbed out.

When she joined him on the sidewalk, he held out his hand. "Ready for this, Mila?"

"Holding hands?"

"Yes, ma'am."

"You bet, cowboy." She linked her fingers through his and they set off down the sidewalk, prompting a few looks and smiles along the way.

Every lamp post along the way was decorated with a Santa hat and a spray of evergreen mixed with holly tied with a red bow. The old-fashioned barber pole in front of Shear Thing wore a Santa hat, too.

Spray snow and painted holiday greetings filled store windows. The traditional life-sized display of Santa's sleigh and his reindeer sat near the gazebo while inside, next to the tree, Santa occupied an ornate throne. A slow-moving line of animated children and their semi-patient parents stretched almost to the street.

A cozy warmth settled in her chest. She'd always dreamed of walking the square at Christmas with a man who appreciated this place as much as she did.

And here he was. "Don't you just love this?" She glanced over at him.

He met her gaze, warmth in his gray eyes. He squeezed her hand. "Sure do."

No doubt about it. This would be the best Christmas ever.

13

The interior of the Mustang Valley General Store was warm compared to the brisk air outside, but Cole shivered as cold sweat trickled down his back. He visualized a mountain meadow and superimposed it over the bustling scene. Christmas was on every aisle and endcap. The carols were nonstop.

He could do this. Had to do this. No way would he ever tell Mila his sob story or let her view him as damaged or abused. His future depended on healing this wound on his own.

"What do you think? Will these work?"

Abandoning his mountain meadow, he forced himself to look at the Santa hats Mila held up. "Sure. Great."

"The felt ones are cheaper than the plush ones, but I don't think they'll look as good."

"Don't worry about the price. I'm buying."

"I'm buying." She smiled. "My idea."

The last thing he needed was an argument. He managed what he hoped was a smile in return. "Then thank you."

"But which do you like? Would the felt ones fit into your old-timey scenario better?"

He swallowed. What had she said? That the felt ones wouldn't look as good as the plush? "Let's go with the plush."

"I think so, too." She peered at him. "Are you okay? You look a little green around the gills."

"Guess I'm hungrier than I thought."

"Well, then, let's get these and get out of here. I'm pretty hungry, myself."

Naturally they had to wait in line. He returned to his mountain meadow visualization and took slow, steady breaths.

"I guess you get quiet when you're hungry."

"Guess so."

"I'll remember that."

An eternity later they were back out on the sidewalk. It was still Christmas there, too, but fresh air helped. How would he do in the Raccoon during lunch? Good time to find out since he'd be there again in a few hours.

He took Mila's hand, careful not to grab it like the lifeline it was. The store filled with everything Christmas — gifts, lights, wrapping paper, bags, bows, and the incessant music — had nearly done him in.

His mother would go shopping a few days before Christmas looking for sales. She'd threaten him and Jordie with no supper if they refused to go and help carry. If it turned out nothing was on sale, she'd stage a public rant in the middle of the store.

Once he'd tried to stop her and she'd backhanded him in front of people he knew. Never tried that again.

Had Mila just said something to him? He checked and she was looking at him, a question in her eyes. "Sorry. I got distracted. You'll have to repeat that."

"You must be *really* hungry."

"Yeah, didn't have much for breakfast. Did you ask me something?"

"Just what you planned to order."

"I'm not sure. How about you?"

She grinned. "Toasted cheese and tomato soup."

"Trying to erase the memory of last night's dinner?"

"Just the opposite! After last night, it's my favorite thing. I want to have it to remind me of how much fun we had."

The knot in his stomach loosened. "But I burned the soup."

"And I fixed it. I thought it tasted just fine. Different, but still tasty. C'mon, admit it."

"I would gladly admit it, but I don't remember what it tasted like. I was too busy watching you watch the Beaver Bunch."

"To quote someone I know, them's kissin' words."

"I know, and I take full responsibility if you can't help yourself."

"You'd let me kiss you right now?"

"Yes, ma'am. Just remember we have a history of things quickly getting out of control."

She tugged on his hand. "Hold still a minute."

"You're gonna?"

"Yes." Holding onto his shoulder, she rose up on her toes and kissed him on the cheek. "There you go."

Looking into her dark eyes, he savored the moist imprint of her lips. Made his skin tingle. He looked into her eyes and the last of his tension melted away. "Thank you. I needed that."

"I had a feeling."

"Did you now?"

"Christmas wasn't very fun for you as a kid, was it?"

His breath caught. "No."

"Luis said this is the first Christmas Jordan has celebrated in a long time."

"Same here."

"Don't worry. I've got you."

His throat tightened. "Thanks." If only it could be that simple. If only having Mila and her loving family could miraculously slay his demons. But they had no idea what they were up against.

"Ready to tie on the feed bag?"

"So ready." As they walked the rest of the way to the Raccoon, he waited for his tension to return. Considering that Clem had put Santa hats on his critters, he'd likely gone all in on the rest of the place.

Sure enough, there was a big ol' silver and gold wreath on the front door. He opened it for Mila and followed her in. The noise level from the lunch crowd nearly drowned out the music from the sound system, soft guitar versions of old carols.

A huge Christmas tree trimmed in gold and silver ribbon with gold and silver-colored musical/themed ornaments stood on the bandstand. Maybe the unusual nature of it kept him from wincing. He'd never seen one dressed up like that.

Clem had continued the gold and silver color scheme throughout the dining area and the bar. Glittering gold and silver angels hung from the rafters and silver vases holding frosted sprigs of evergreen sat on each table.

The absence of traditional red and green soothed him in ways he couldn't explain. He let out a sigh.

"I had the same reaction," Mila said. "The only red in the whole place is those Santa hats on the raccoons. There's something so peaceful about these decorations."

"Maybe it's the music."

"I'm sure that's part of it. That much will change tonight when the Rooty Toots get up there." She turned toward the slim redhead coming toward them. "Hi, Julie. Congrats on becoming dining room manager."

"Thanks! I'm happy about it."

"Got a table for two?"

"Sure do. Hey, Cole, haven't seen you in here in a while."

Cole smiled at her, impressed that she remembered his name. "Keeping busy out at the ranch. Congrats on your promotion."

"Thank you. You're coming tonight, I hope, and bringing your fiddle."

"I am."

"Folks love hearing you play."

"I'm glad. It's fun for me, too." Wow, here he was in the middle of a venue decorated for

Christmas and having a normal, relaxed conversation. It gave him hope.

Once they were seated and had placed their order, Julie left. Mila leaned toward him, her dark eyes sparkling. "She asks me about you all the time. Definitely has a crush going on."

"Then maybe you should give me another kiss on the cheek."

"I would, but for sure I'd knock over this lovely centerpiece. I think if we spend our time gazing into each other's eyes she'll get the picture."

"That'll be easy. I just do that naturally."

"You're feeling better, aren't you?"

"Better?"

"When we were in the store I thought you were going to throw up."

He shoved down a wave of panic. "That's what I get for eating a hard-boiled egg that's been sitting there too long." Another white lie.

"Seriously?"

"There might have been some mold on the bagel, too."

"Cole! You're not a human compost bin."

"You're the one who said food shouldn't go to waste." His conscience pricked him, but the truth would take them down a road he refused to travel.

"But you still shouldn't eat it if it's spoiled. FYI, my mom has a compost pile. Next time take that stuff to her. You might want to go through your fridge and weed out what's gone bad."

"You could come in with me when we get back and we could go through it together."

Her gaze softened. "Wish I could. I promised Greta I'd do her hair and that'll take a while. Just don't snack on anything iffy. I'm planning for us to have a really good time tonight."

"I'm planning for us to have a really good time the next morning. Early the next morning." He was ready to ditch the subject of spoiled food.

She flushed. "Watch yourself. We're still very much in the public eye."

"Are we? I can't see anybody but you."

"You're certainly good for my ego."

This was more like it. "You're good for every part of me, some more than others."

Her flush deepened. "Honestly, I can't take you anywhere."

"Not without violating some public decency laws." He paused, waiting for that to register. When her breath caught, he smiled. "But that still leaves us with a lot of possibilities."

She rolled her eyes, but her pink cheeks and unsteady breath gave her away. "Clearly the effects of that rotten egg and moldy bagel have worn off and your mind has returned to its favorite topic."

"Which is you."

"Not just me. It's me and a certain activity."

"No, it's just you." He dropped the teasing. This was important. "I would be happy if all we did was sit and play checkers."

"Fully clothed?"

"Fully clothed. Just being in the same space, breathing the same air."

She regarded him steadily. "I think you mean that."

"You have no idea how much I mean that." Someday she would know. He just had to make it through Christmas without falling apart.

14

When Mila inherited the mini-hacienda from her grandmother, she'd invited Claudie to share it. Since then, Greta had come over the afternoon of the Raccoon Christmas party so they could get dressed together and Mila could do her hair. After their dad died, their mom had decided to tag along.

They arrived at four and were still hanging up their coats when Greta burst out with, "What's the deal with Cole? Are you two..." She paused to make air quotes. "*Involved*?"

Claudie sent Mila a wide-eyed look. "I promise I didn't tell—"

"I know you didn't." Her cheeks grew warm, which she *hated*. She was thirty years old, for fudge sake. But making love with Cole was so rambunctious and thrilling that thinking about it made her entire body flush.

"Rio told us," Greta said. "He came over to snitch some Christmas cookies this morning. To hear him tell it, he interrupted a make-out session in the woods near the front gate."

Great. So now she was even redder. And couldn't look her mother in the eye.

Claudie started laughing. "Oh, my."

"That's all the evidence I need." Greta glanced at Claudie. "And you already knew?"

"I did."

Greta zeroed in on Mila. "Spill it."

"Yes, we're involved." She gathered her forces and lifted her chin. "And I'm very happy about it."

"Me, too!" Greta raced over and gave her a hug. "We've been hoping you'd get together ever since the wedding."

"We?"

"Mom and me. We've talked about it a *lot*."

Mila finally met her mother's amused gaze. "Really?"

"I wouldn't say a *lot*, *mija*, but you two made such a cute couple at the reception — Cole playing his fiddle and you doing the vocals. I thought that would be the tipping point, but I guess not."

"We...um...we weren't ready."

"But then he invited you over to see his secret project." Greta's cheeks dimpled in a teasing grin. "Was that the tipping point?"

"In a way."

"Aha! So now you can tell us about that project, right?"

"No, I can't."

"What?" Her little sister grabbed her again. "But we're your nearest and dearest! And we're champion secret keepers."

"It'll be a way better surprise if you know nothing before you see it."

"But that won't be until *Christmas*. C'mon, give us a hint."

"Nope."

"Last night she let it slip that it moved," Claudie said, "and that Dad would have loved it."

"*Dios*." Their mother threw up her hands. "Please tell me it's not a gate. There's nothing your papa loved more than gates but enough is enough."

"He loved you more than gates, *Mamacita*." Greta gave her a side hug.

"*Un poquito*," Her smile was bittersweet.

"It's not a gate," Claudie said. "And it's not a zombie Santa or those sparkly deer statues people put in their yards."

"Could be some sort of animated Christmas scene, though." Greta tucked her hands in her pockets and rocked back on her heels. "But I thought it was gonna be a year-round thing." She peered at Mila. "Is it?"

"I'm not saying."

"You know we won't let on that you told us."

"Doesn't matter. It's Cole's secret, not mine, and I promised not to reveal it."

"That's the end of it, then." Their mother's command was softly spoken. Whenever she gave them that look, she didn't need volume to convey her message. "Breaking a promise is a terrible way to begin a relationship."

"Right, Mama." Greta picked up the tote she'd brought in. "We'd better get dressed. Wouldn't want to keep my big sister's *novio* waiting." Flashing Mila a smile , she headed down the hall.

Mila expected more teasing from her sisters as everyone put on their Christmas-themed party clothes, spent extra time on their hair and added glamorous touches to their makeup. She didn't mind the teasing.

They only did it because they liked Cole and approved of this matchup. Nobody in her family had warmed to her last boyfriend. She'd rationalized that once they got to know him, they would thaw.

Never happened. They'd sensed what she'd refused to see. But Cole had won everyone's heart from the get-go, including hers. Her family's stamp of approval said a lot about his character.

Her anticipation for the evening ahead kept building until she felt like a shaken bottle of champagne. By the time Cole rapped on the front door, she ran to open it while her sisters and mom giggled in the background.

She flung it open and sucked in a breath. "Wow." She moved back and ushered him in.

"Wow, yourself." His gaze traveled from her glittering red boots to the sparkling hairclip she'd used to hold back one side of her hair. "That dress looks gorgeous on you."

"Thank you. You look gorgeous all over."

He chuckled. "So do you."

The glow in his eyes justified every penny she'd spent on the fringed, winter-white dress she'd bought months ago specifically for this party. Last night's epic lovemaking had made her forget the party and the dress.

As if they'd planned it, he wore a snow-white yoked western shirt with silver embroidery.

She'd seen those jet-black dress jeans once before, at the wedding. "Have you worn that shirt before?"

"No, ma'am. Jordie brought it over an hour ago. She said to tell you she's very pleased about... you know."

"We're pleased, too!" Greta sang out.

His attention shifted and he whipped off his hat. "My apologies, ladies. Didn't intend to ignore you." Pink tinged his cheeks. "I—"

"You only have eyes for Mila." Greta gave the line a dramatic lilt. "No insult taken. We understand."

"You all know?"

"Because of Rio," Mila said.

Right on cue, the door opened and her rumor-spreading little brother poked his head in. "Y'all ready? Cole left the truck running and gas doesn't grow on trees, y'know."

"We're coming, Mr. Tattletale." Claudie grabbed jackets off the coat tree and handed them out.

Rio chuckled. "Can't help it if Sol is nuts about me. Blame him for telling on you guys. Nice dress, Mila. Have I seen that before?"

"Nope." She put her arms in the suede jacket Cole held for her.

"Classy. Looks like something Auntie Kat would like."

"She's the one who told me to buy it."

"See? Knew it."

"Hey, *mijo*." Their mom made a shooing motion with her hand. "In or out. Electricity doesn't grow on trees, either."

"I'm out. I'll be in the truck. In the backseat, of course." He started to close the door, then opened it again. "The rest of you look awesome, too. Nice up-do, Gret." He closed the door.

"Little brothers," Claudie mumbled. "Can't live with 'em, can't live without 'em."

"I'm glad he caught us." Mila buttoned her coat. "Now Cole and I can act natural. It'll be more fun this way."

"I agree." Cole glanced around. "Looks like we're all ready to—"

A horn blared from somewhere outside.

Claudie started for the door. "Rio Bridger, so help me—"

"That's not my horn," Cole said. "I think it's—"

"The van's horn?" Raquel laughed. "Of course it is. We'd better get a move on, Greta. The Dazzling Damsels are ready to party." She started for the door. "Which reminds me, Cole, are you taking your fiddle?"

"It's in the truck."

"Excellent. Tia Ezzie would've been heartbroken if you'd decided not to play tonight. She's hoping you know *Feliz Navidad.*"

"If Mila can sing it for me I can probably manage it." He glanced her way.

"I'll be glad to."

"Ezzie will be thrilled. We'll see you kids there." She and Greta hurried out and closed the door behind them.

"You two go ahead." Claudie made a shooing motion. "I need to turn off the Christmas trees."

"Oh, right!" Mila looked at Cole. "I'll bet you didn't even notice them with all that was going on."

"No, but I can check them out now." He swung around and surveyed the trees, a big one by the front window, medium-sized trees on either side of the fireplace a safe distance away from any flames, and a small one on the coffee table. "Very nice. Must have taken a lot of time."

"We love doing it." Claudie switched off the lights on the largest one. "One of our favorite things. Okay, go ahead. I've got this."

As Cole held the door, Mila took a mental picture of his handsome self, her date for the night. Yum. "Is anyone else riding with us besides Rio?"

"Yes, ma'am. Monty." He closed the door, took her hand and headed for the truck parked outside the low wall surrounding the front patio.

Claudie caught up with them. "Did I just hear you say Monty's going with us?"

"He is."

"Then I'll talk to him about Pickles, who's favoring his right front foot."

Mila chuckled. "And keep him talking so he won't fall asleep?"

"Bingo."

"Is that a possibility?" Cole sounded surprised.

"Always is if he's a passenger," Mila said.

"And when he sleeps, he leans," Claudie added as Rio climbed out of the truck. "Traditionally I'm in the middle because my legs are shorter."

"As it happens, I don't have that tradition in my truck." Cole squeezed Mila's hand and let go as he approached Rio. "Go ahead and hop in, buddy. That way we can make sure Claudie doesn't wrinkle her skirt on the drive in."

"You bet, Cole. Good thinking." Rio hopped in the truck and took the middle seat.

Claudie leaned toward Mila. "Hang onto this one."

"I plan to." She waited while Cole helped her sister in. Instead of standing there, she could've climbed up on her own, but accepting a gallant gesture from a sexy guy in a Stetson was more fun.

He took care to make sure no part of her fringed skirt was in danger before gifting her with a smile and closing the door.

The little girl in her felt like a princess on her way to a ball where she'd dance with the prince. The woman in her savored the reality of heading to a party at a country-western bar where she'd dance with a dashing cowboy. And at the end of the night, she and the cowboy would make sweet love.

Whoever said you can't have it all hadn't met Cole Sterling.

<u>15</u>

When Cole walked into his first ever Christmas party with his fiddle case in hand and Mila by his side, he took heart. The noise level and general merriment stood a good chance of buffering the crappy memories that had haunted him all his life.

Sticking with Mila would help, too. He was glad that she'd chosen a dress that was Christmas-adjacent rather than on the nose. No embroidered candy canes, reindeer, Santa or decorated trees. Just a slinky white dress on a woman with the curves to make the most of it.

A quick glance at the hair clip holding her lustrous hair behind her right ear had indicated it was a jeweled wreath. He chose not to look closely. He'd rather focus on her mouth, anyway.

Dealing with her intense sensual appeal distracted him from all the holiday outfits everyone else had on, including the members of the Rooty Toots. With a little imagination, he could see this as just another night out at a country-western bar.

Luckily there hadn't been much Christmas music in his parents' house, just plenty of fighting as they blamed each other for their poverty. They fought about it all year but the arguments turned vicious at Christmas, the season of giving.

Soon after he parked his fiddle case on the bandstand and got settled with Mila at one of the Bridger tables, the Rooty Toots launched into a brisk version of *Deck the Halls.* Inviting Mila to dance, he plunged into the fray, taking Mila out on the floor for a fast two-step. Might as well jump into the deep end and find out if he could swim.

She laughed as he spun her under his arm and the fringe on her sleeve tickled his cheek. "Getting right into it, are we?"

"Yes, ma'am." He pulled her close for a tantalizing second and then twirled her around again. "Like it?"

"Love it." Happiness gleamed in her dark eyes.

Just what he was going for. He'd keep his demons at bay no matter what it took. For Mila.

He'd never danced to a Christmas carol before. The uniqueness of it added another layer of protection against those fudging ghouls that stalked him this time of year.

Her dress had fringe down the side seams as well as on the sleeves. Watching her hips as she made that fringe shimmy filled his head with thoughts so hot they banished the ghosts of Christmas past. He could do this.

Rooty Toot was clearly on fire. They followed up with another fast one, a rocking version of *God Rest Ye, Merry Gentlemen.* He tugged Mila back on the floor. Adrenaline was his friend tonight.

She was panting by the time they finished the number. "Enough. I need to—"

As if the band had heard her plea, they switched to *Silent Night* played as a waltz.

He slid his hand behind her back. "Will this do?"

"Yes." Holding his gaze, she fell into step with the slow, gliding pace. "Waltzing makes me feel like a princess."

"You look like one in that dress."

"I bought it in October. Tia Kat talked me into it."

"I'm glad she did. Was that before or after the wedding?"

"After. She told me if I wanted to catch a certain cowboy, this was the dress that would do the trick."

"A *certain* cowboy?"

"You, of course."

Mila's Auntie Kat had been on his side since October? Nice to know. "The dress looks great on you, but you didn't need to put in extra effort. I was hooked a long time ago."

She grinned. "Then let's call it icing on the cake."

"A very spicy cake it is, too. I like the flavor." And he was getting hungrier by the second.

"Mama thought we might get together after the wedding. I told her we weren't ready then. The timing had to be right."

"Considering how ready I am right now, I think we might have overshot the mark." He pulled her closer. "How much longer before we can go home?"

She smiled. "Silly man. We just got here."

"Then I need to step outside and find me a handful of snow."

Her smile widened. "That was the funniest—"

"Hey, you two." Luis whirled Jordie around only a couple of feet away. "Adam's ordering food so you need to go find him after this dance."

"Thanks," Cole called back. "But we can—"

"It's easier if he puts in one order," Mila said. "You have two choices—beef stew or chili."

"I like 'em both, but why only two?"

"Easy on the kitchen and affordable for the customers. Clem's got this down to a science."

"Then I should just slip Adam some cash later for the bill?"

"The business pays for it. Simpler that way."

"Ah." He supposed it was, but while Clem was providing a reasonably priced meal, the Bridger Bunch was sixteen strong at last count. The bill would be sizeable.

Maybe not to them, though. He only had a vague idea of how much money the family had. Yeah, they owned around twenty thousand acres, but ranchers could be land rich and cash poor.

He had a hunch that wasn't the case with the Bridger Bunch. He wasn't going to let their wealth intimidate him because that kind of thinking would screw up his relationship with Mila real fast. Still, the contrast between his upbringing and hers was breathtaking.

Silent Night came to a sweet close and he allowed himself to bring Mila in for a hug. "That was nice."

"More than nice." She gazed up at him. "Dancing with you is a joy. I knew it would be wonderful, but it's even better than I imagined."

"Yeah, I'm thinking we should make a habit of driving in to go dancing." Then he heard what he'd just said, and the assumption lying beneath it — that they were a couple now and would be spending most of their time together. "I mean, it's an idea, but—"

"It's a terrific idea." The music started up again. "We should get off the floor before we're run over."

"Good point." He reluctantly let her go and they moved over near the bar.

Turning toward him, she rested her palms on his chest. "I want to be with you, Cole. I want to plan things with you. Dancing, horseback rides, movies, lunch in town. Don't hold back. Don't second-guess yourself. This is real."

Sliding his hands around her waist, he let out a sigh of relief. "It is for me."

"For me, too. And now we need to find Adam and tell him what we want."

"If I tell him what I want right now he'll punch me in the face."

"What we want for *dinner.*"

"I know. I'm just messing with you." Tucking her against his side, he scanned the crowd. "I see him. Let's go put in our order. Since I can't have what I really want, guess I'll have to settle for chili."

He kept his tone light, but there was nothing light about this moment. Mila wanted to be with him, and not just for sex. That was huge.

Life had never been this good. Jordie was right. He'd spent a lifetime short-changing himself. That habit ended now.

16

Luis and Jordan invited them to share a table and Mila jumped at the chance to spend time with her brother and sister-in-law. They'd been super busy lately due to the success of the Jordan Sterling Equestrian Center.

Back in July Luis had proposed building an indoor arena as a winter venue for Jordan's clinics and his wild horse training program. Cole had led the crew that completed the main structure before the wedding, which had been held there.

Now the arena was fully functional, providing Jordan and Luis with more business than they could handle. Mila was thrilled about that, but she couldn't remember the last time she'd had a relaxed conversation with either of them.

Drinks had been ordered and delivered by the time she settled in across the table from Jordan, who was sporting a new look. The blonde hair that used to reach to the middle of her back was now shoulder-length. Before Mila could say how much she liked it, Jordan beat her to the punch.

"Yay for you guys, getting all lovey-dovey on the dance floor. I've been so hoping this would happen."

"And we have you to thank," Cole said. "If you hadn't come to town on the Fourth, Mila and I would never have met."

Luis smiled at Jordan. "I'm pretty happy about that decision, myself."

"Yeah, well, there was a point where I thought I'd made a gigantic mistake. But now that you two have figured out you're perfect for each other and I've settled in with this guy...." She gazed fondly at Luis. "I'll take credit for making a fudging brilliant move."

"I'll drink to that." Cole lifted his mug of ginger ale in her direction. "I owe you, sis, and the Bridger Bunch for taking me in. Just saying thanks doesn't seem like enough, though."

"Hey, you built us an arena." Luis picked up his bottle of Modelo. "We need to toast that. Everyone said it would take at least six months just to build the enclosure. You finished in less than three and came in under budget."

"We absolutely need to toast that," Jordan said. "I knew you were good, big brother, but I didn't know you were a miracle worker."

"I had a great crew. I don't know who taught everyone in this family how to swing a hammer, but—"

"That was Dad," Luis said.

"Obviously he knew his stuff. With the family pitching in and my two buddies from work taking it on as a side job, it was a snap to finish ahead of schedule. As for the budget, the lumber yard prices looked like a Bridger discount to me."

Mila gave him a nudge. "All those things may be true, but it was your leadership that supplied the rocket fuel."

"I had ulterior motives. I wanted to see my sis get married in a place I helped build."

"I loved seeing the family come together to make that deadline." Luis sounded wistful. "It was like the old days with Dad."

Mila nodded. "It was. And Jordan and Cole have no idea what we mean."

"True." He looked across the table at Cole. "Our dad had a pattern. First he'd ask a contactor friend to estimate how much time a project would take and then bust ass to beat that estimate."

"And bust our asses if we were working on it with him," Mila added.

"Yeah, but nobody complained. We wanted to beat the odds, too. The point is, gratitude goes both ways, Cole. We're thankful, too."

"I appreciate that, but if you need any major work done on your casita, I hope you'll let me know."

Luis exchanged a look with Jordan, who gave a slight nod. He turned back to Cole. "As it happens, we'll be adding another bedroom as soon as the weather warms up. I could use a hand with that if you're available."

"You're adding on?" Mila's gaze locked with her brother's as a potential reason popped into her head. "How come?"

His dark eyes sparkled. "Seems we need more space. We could convert the guest room, but instead we—"

"A baby?" She said it softly, figuring the music would cover her words in case she was wrong. She didn't want to start a stampede.

"Uh-huh." His grin took up his whole face.

"*Madre mia!*" Leaping up, she ran around the table to grab hold of them and collided with Cole, who'd come from the other side.

Jordan_cracked up. "This is the most disorganized group hug in the history of group hugs."

"That's what you get for springing it on us. Awesome news, sis." Cole gave her a kiss on the cheek and reached over to shake Luis's hand. "What's the due date?"

"And who else did you tell?" Mila let go of them and stepped back.

"She's due in July," Luis said. "And Mama knows. So does Greta, since it would've been mean to make her leave the room."

"Yeah, it would've." She was touched that she'd been next in line after their mother. She would have been okay if he'd gone to Adam next, but he'd chosen her. The bond forged in their complicated childhood remained strong. Jordan clearly felt the same about Cole.

Luis glanced past Cole and rose from his chair. "And here comes the family."

Adam, Tracy and Claudie hurried over. Claudie was in the lead, but Adam spoke first. "Hey, bro, got something to tell us?"

"You guys were next on the list. Mila blew my cover." Luis went to meet them. "We're having a baby."

Claudie squealed and threw herself at Luis, then headed for Jordan.

"Wow." Adam looked thunderstruck. "That's...that's..." Abandoning his search for words, he pulled Luis into a fierce hug. Then he let him go as he dragged in a breath and turned to Jordan. "You both look so happy." His voice was gruff with emotion.

"We are." Jordan's blue eyes glistened as Adam embraced her.

"I'm getting choked up." Tracy's voice sounded clogged as she hugged Luis and then held out her arms to Jordan. "What an unexpected and fabulous Christmas gift."

"An unexpected gift?" Rio arrived, followed by Zay and Monty. "My guess is either a baby or a winning lottery ticket. I can't say which is better, but—"

"A baby, doofus." Zay gave him a punch on the arm. "The lottery's just money. A baby makes you an uncle."

"Hey, it does, doesn't it? That would be super cool. Which is it, bro?"

"Baby."

"Excellent!" He hugged Luis and Jordan before turning around and high-fiving Zay and Monty. "Uncles! We're all gonna be uncles!"

"Move aside, boys. Move aside." Tia Kat parted the group with a wave of her hand, making way for Grandma Doris, Tia Carmen and Tia Ezzie. "*Las ninaras* have arrived."

Cole leaned toward Mila as the Dazzling Damsels fussed over Luis and Jordan. "What's *ninaras* mean?"

"Babysitters."

He chuckled. "Nice. This is gonna be one lucky kid."

"You have no idea. Mama must be over the—"

"Hey, Bridger Bunch!" someone called out from the crowd. "Sounds like baby news over there. Care to confirm it?"

Luis glanced at Jordan. "Should we announce it to the crowd?"

She laughed. "Might as well."

"Believe I will." He headed for the bandstand where the Rooty Toots had just finished playing *Run, Run, Rudolph*.

Hopping up on the stage, he took the mic Sam handed him. "As most of you have probably guessed, Jordan and I just got the best Christmas news ever." He paused to suck in a breath. "Next July we'll have a baby!"

The crowd erupted in cheers and the Rooty Toots started playing Amy Grant's *Baby, Baby*. Folks left their seats and made tracks for the Bridger Bunch gathered around Jordan.

At the outpouring of love from friends and neighbors, Mila's stalwart brother who mostly kept his emotions to himself, ducked his head to thumb tears from his eyes. Which brought tears to her eyes. Then a strong hand reached for her, drawing her close.

Cole's image was a little blurry but his warm arm around her waist communicated more than words that he treasured this special moment. She blinked and her vision cleared. Glancing up, she met his gaze. Call her crazy, but this man looked an awful lot like her future.

17

Cole wasn't surprised about the baby. His sister adored Luis and Laughing Creek Ranch. A baby made perfect sense.

Sure did shine a different light on his own situation, though. He'd left his old life behind, determined to create a more meaningful existence. Mila was a step in that direction.

But his feelings were all over the place — awe, gratitude, anxiety... love? They hadn't touched on that one yet.

He'd never been here before, poised on the brink of committing to a woman. But that wasn't the whole picture, was it?

Mila wanted kids. He didn't even have to ask. Her reaction to this announcement told him all he needed to know. And suddenly he was staring down a concept that scared the hell out of him.

Judging from the way his little sis basked in the warmth of the Bridger Bunch, she'd banished the crippling memories of their childhood. He envied that.

Eventually everyone meandered back to their respective tables and food began to arrive.

Not surprisingly, Mila was more focused on the baby than her meal. "I can't *wait* for July. Wouldn't it be something if he or she showed up on the Fourth?"

"We're counting on it," Luis said. "She'll arrive on the Fourth and we'll name her Liberty."

"Smart move, choosing a gender-neutral name. You could have a boy, you know."

"Possible but unlikely. We both think we'll have a girl."

"Alrighty, then. I'll look forward to meeting my niece on the Fourth of July. Will that be before the parade or after?"

Jordie grinned. "Or during. Luis already assigned me to the wagon with Grandma and the Aunties."

"Sounds like my first parade's gonna be a doozy." Cole picked up a piece of the cornbread that had come with his chili. "Will you be taking this munchkin on the road?"

She nodded. "Not right away, though. It'll probably be the following spring, when we return to our regular clinic schedule. But thanks to our lovely arena here, we'll still be in business in the meantime."

"We can also concentrate more on the rehabilitation side, bring in more candidates." Luis took a sip of his Modelo. "That's more flexible."

"And it turns out I love that process." Jordie tipped her bowl to spoon up the last of her stew. "Gaining a wild animal's trust is such a thrill." She glanced at Cole. "You'd like it, too. Since we'll be hanging around more, maybe you could go out with us sometimes."

"I would like that. Here we are living so close, but we're like ships passing in the night."

She sent him a teasing glance. "Especially since you started your secret project."

"Yeah, I know."

"In fact, we haven't even danced together since you moved here." She put down her bowl. "Come on. Let's show Luis and Mila our fancy footwork."

He abandoned the rest of his chili and pushed back his chair. "Great idea."

"Get him to tell you about the project," Luis called out as they left the table.

"Not my plan!" She led the way to the dance floor.

Cole chuckled. "You sure?"

"Yep. I wanted to check on you." She moved into his arms as they executed a brisk two-step.

"Why?"

She lowered her voice. "You're freaking out about this baby."

"Does it show?"

"Not to anyone else. But I can tell."

"Keep it to yourself." The lively dance only allowed for short sentences.

"You know I will."

"It's just that I didn't think about..."

"Mila wanting babies someday?"

"Yep." He twirled her under his arm. "I can't picture being a dad."

"I couldn't picture being a mom." She spun around again. "This family changes you."

"What if I turn into our dad?"

"It'll never happen." She followed him as he executed a tricky step. "I won't let you."

"Good to know."

"Besides, he wasn't as bad as Mom. She hit us."

His veins turned to ice. Stumbling, he almost stepped on her toes.

"Cole?"

"Sorry. Out of practice."

She gave him a look, clearly not buying it.

He pretended not to notice and concentrated on his footwork. He'd shielded her all his life and wasn't about to stop now.

"Mila can help you."

"With my dancing?"

"With your PTSD."

"I don't have—"

"Yes, you do. We both do."

His jaw tightened. A label would only make it worse.

"Luis is my saving grace. Mila can be yours."

"She doesn't need to hear my sob story."

"She wouldn't see it like that."

He begged to differ. Mila wasn't into guys with sob stories. She'd told him as much.

"I believe we're meant to be here, with this family."

"I'm sure you are, sis."

"You are, too."

"Hope so." He'd been more confident earlier, but now he was second-guessing the whole program.

"How're you doing with Christmas?"

"Okay." It was sort of true.

"They all think your project is a Christmas present."

"I know."

"They're all giving you stuff."

He sighed. "I was afraid of that."

"You haven't told them not to?"

"No. Have you?"

"Didn't have the heart."

"Did you buy them presents?"

"I did. Something for you, too."

He groaned. "But I didn't—"

"You're covered. You have a group gift."

He sighed again. "Not my intention."

"The timing is perfect. How'd that happen?"

"It crept up on me."

"Then Mila doesn't know how much you loathe—"

"She doesn't, and please don't tell—"

"I wouldn't, big brother."

"What have you said to Luis?"

"Not much. He knows I'm not a fan."

"But you have lights and presents."

"He loves this time of year."

"And you love him."

"Exactly." The song ended. Meeting his gaze, she patted him on the chest. "Just get through Christmas. It'll be clear sledding after that."

"I'll follow your lead." At least until the twenty-fourth. Then he would go underground with some excuse or other.

During the time he and Jordie had lived together, they'd stayed in that night watching reruns of *Bonanza*. If she'd noticed that he'd quietly gotten drunk every Christmas Eve, she'd never commented on it.

That was still his preferred method of handling the occasion. Assuming he came up with a decent cover story, he'd be able to do the same this year.

But as he escorted his sister back to the table, Mila glanced away from her conversation with Luis and gave him a heart-melting smile. Guilt sat like a lump of moldy cheese in his gut.

Was he seriously planning to lie to her about his reasons for skipping Christmas Eve with her family? Sure looked like it.

The alternative was treating her to the ugly story he'd never told anyone. He wasn't about to risk it. He could come off looking like the manipulative SOB she'd dumped. Or even worse, a damaged man who wasn't worthy of her.

18

"I'm happy for you, *mana*." As Jordan and Cole headed to the dance floor, Luis settled back in his chair with a sigh of contentment. "This thing with Cole seems right."

"It feels right." Mila gazed at him. "Like it was supposed to be."

"Funny how it worked out. If Jordan had been willing to date me when I attended that clinic with her five years ago, you still might have met her brother."

"But we weren't the same people five years ago. We might not have clicked."

"But they both would've met Dad."

"Yeah. I hate that they didn't get to."

"And he didn't get to meet them." He fell silent. "Or Liberty."

Pain sliced into her heart. "I'm so sorry."

"Me, too." He dragged in a breath. "It really bothered me, but you and Cole getting together helps. It helps a lot."

"I'm glad, but I don't see why—"

"If Dad hadn't died, we wouldn't have needed to hire Cole."

"Huh. I guess not."

"I'm not saying the four of us wouldn't have ended up here, but—"

"I don't think we would have. Change one thing and everything changes."

"Exactly." Luis's attention shifted to the dance floor. "They look cute out there. We're supposed to be watching so we'd better do that."

"We should."

"Jordan said they took lessons together during the time she shared his apartment. They're really close."

"They are. I like that." The rush of excitement over the baby news was fading, giving her more perspective on Cole's mood. He'd been excited, too, but thinking back on it, he'd also looked vaguely uneasy about this turn of events.

Then Jordan had asked him to dance. Mila would bet her share of the family Yule log that Jordan had wanted to check on him. They weren't having a barrel of laughs during that two-step, which indicated a discussion could be taking place.

It might be a sister-brother thing that had nothing to do with her. But what if her joyful response to the baby news had given the impression she couldn't wait to have her own? Wouldn't hurt to set the record straight.

She wouldn't get the chance anytime soon, though. As soon as Cole and Jordan returned to the table, they had company. Sam, the band's lead guitarist, appeared armed with sheet music in hand.

He and Cole went into a huddle while they discussed it. Then Sam returned to the bandstand, stepped up to the mic and faced the crowd. "Who's ready for some top-notch fiddle playing?"

The enthusiastic response put a smile on Cole's face that was beautiful to see. The lines of tension around his eyes disappeared as he rose to his feet and headed to the bandstand accompanied by eager applause.

While he pulled his fiddle from its case, Sam set up a metal stand for the sheet music. Mila's assumption that Cole only played by ear was dead wrong. He'd put more into this endeavor than he'd let on.

She shouldn't be surprised. He wasn't the type to do anything halfway. Taking a pair of reading glasses from his fiddle case, he scanned the music, then tucked the glasses away.

Mila glanced at Jordan. "Does he have a photographic memory?"

"Pretty much. I think he had the tendency and built on it because he hates wearing glasses, especially when he's playing."

Sam adjusted his guitar strap over his shoulder and moved up to the mic again. "You're welcome to dance to this, folks, but it might be tricky. I suggest just sitting back and giving us a listen." He glanced at Cole. "Ready, buddy?"

"Let's do it."

"Then here's our version of *Carol of the Bells.*"

The music began, and Mila went very still. Always before Cole had performed in a casual, playful way, with an almost careless disregard for the process. He had knowingly or accidentally disguised...*this.*

His intense focus showed in every line of his body, every stroke of his bow as the soaring melody poured from his violin. The breathtaking river of emotion swirled through the room, mesmerizing everyone in it.

Conversation stopped. Forks were put down, drinks abandoned. Not a chair scraped as everyone sat enthralled by the majestic, hypnotizing sound.

The guitars formed the base of the piece, while the violin created the achingly sweet top notes, moving faster, higher, and faster yet. The tempo increased, finally building to a crescendo that filled the air with glory.

Cole's bow flew, a blur of motion as the guitars kept pace.... And it was done! Cole plucked the final notes. Ding...dong. Ding...dong.

A moment of awed silence ended when the room erupted with a standing ovation. The band members and Cole bowed and exchanged grins, clearly proud of themselves.

Sam leaned toward the mic. "Always wanted to try that. Never had a fiddle player who was up to it. Let's hear it for Cole Sterling!"

As everyone whooped and hollered, Cole blushed and tipped his hat.

"And now that we've got him up here, I intend to keep him for a while. Get back out on the floor folks, for a change of pace. Here's *Rockin' Around the Christmas Tree!*"

Cole might not have known the tune, but he got through it just fine. Same with the next one. In a way she was relieved that he didn't need her up there with him. Singing at this event was a much bigger deal than it had been at the wedding.

Good thing she'd enjoyed a couple of dances with the guy earlier, though. Might be some time before she'd have the opportunity again.

She had fun as usual, dancing with her brothers and chatting with friends. Tia Kat started a conga line, a years-old tradition of winding through the tables and passing out hugs to those who'd chosen to sit it out.

When the Rooty Toots finally took a break and Cole headed back to the table, Mila figured this was her cue. She waited while he remained standing, gulping down some water and responding to comments about *Carol of the Bells*.

When he started to take a seat, she left her chair. "Could I talk you into going for a walk?"

His eyebrows lifted as if she'd suggested taking a rocket ship to the moon. "Outside?"

"Sure. There's no wind tonight and the square holds in the heat. It's not as cold as walking around out on the ranch. It'll be lovely."

"You should do it," Jordan said. "It sounds very winter-wonderlandish."

Luis stood, too. "Does that mean you want to go, too?"

"I'd rather stay here and order dessert. That's romantic, too."

"Then I'll order us some." He glanced at Mila. "Want me to get you two something for when you get back?"

"Not for me, thanks. Want dessert, Cole?"

"Not right now, thanks. Maybe later." He grabbed his coat and hers. "Off we go."

"Hey, Cole!" Sam called out as they walked away. "Hope you're not leaving. We're hoping for more fiddle music after the break."

"I'll be back!" He gave them a wave and continued toward the front door with Mila. He lowered his voice. "Unless you have other plans."

"I wouldn't dream of taking you away from your fans." She pushed her arms into the sleeves of the coat he held for her. "Besides, you're the designated driver. You can't leave early."

"Something I realized after the fact."

"You probably think I'm nuts inviting you out into the cold." She buttoned her coat and turned up the thick shearling collar.

"No, ma'am." He put on his jacket and repositioned his hat, tugging on the brim. "I'm sure you have a good reason for suggesting this walk."

"I do."

"If it involves kissing, I'm all in."

Warmth flooded her body. "It just might." What the heck. Her lipstick was mostly gone, anyway.

"Then let's go." He ushered her out the door.

When she stepped out of the noisy tavern into the quiet night, she let out a sigh. "I love these parties, but...."

"This is a great idea." Wrapping his arm around her waist, he tucked her against him. "Which way?"

"Let's walk over to the gazebo."

"Better yet, we could walk around behind the gazebo." He matched his stride to hers as they stepped off the curb and walked across the deserted street.

"To be clear, I didn't suggest this just so we could make out." Her boots crunched on a thin layer of snow as they headed toward the glittering focal point of the town square.

"That's too bad."

"I need to clarify something."

"Go for it."

"I'm not a ticking clock."

"Huh?"

"Some people think... I mean, it's kind of a cliché but—"

"Oh." He cleared his throat. "I get it. The baby thing."

Pausing, she faced him, slid her arms around his neck and tucked her hands under his collar. "I'm excited for Luis and Jordan, but I'm not jealous. Their announcement didn't create a burning desire to get pregnant ASAP."

His gaze searched hers. "Okay."

"I wondered if you might assume that was the case. I fit the profile. I'm over thirty. And now we've made love, so—"

"I didn't think that. I can't imagine you wanting to rush into motherhood when we've just started this thing. It would be totally out of character."

"Thank you." The knot in her chest loosened. "I was afraid all my gushing sent the wrong message. I'm glad you didn't take it that way. Let's just forget I said any—"

"But since you brought it up, I should probably let you know where I stand on the subject."

Her breath caught. "That sounds ominous."

"I don't mean it to be, but..." He sighed. "Although you won't ask me to ditch the condoms tonight, it hit me that someday you will."

Her chest tightened again. "And that's a problem?"

"Yeah."

"You don't want kids?"

"It's not that I don't want them. It's that I probably shouldn't have them."

"Why?"

"I didn't have the greatest role model. I don't trust myself to—"

"You don't? When you've been such an amazing big brother to Jordan?"

"Not the same."

"Not exactly, but—"

"What I'm trying to say is that much as I've enjoyed every second we've been together, much as I want to keep that up, we need to face the fact that—"

"I can guess what you're about to say and it's fudging nonsense. You—"

"I'm not a good prospect in the long run. You need someone who—"

"I need you." She ducked under his hat and laid one on him, gripping the back of his neck and not letting go until he groaned and started kissing her back.

When he shifted to take the kiss deeper, he knocked his hat to the frozen ground. She tried to pull away and retrieve it, but he tugged her closer. Thrusting his fingers into her hair, he held her head as he continued to ravish her mouth.

Desire pulsed in her core. She whimpered, craving what his kisses promised, aching for the heat of his body to meld with hers.

Gasping, he broke away from the kiss. "This is insane. If anyone looks out the windows...."

"Do you care?"

"No. Do you?"

"No."

"That's all I need to hear." He quickly undid his jacket buttons and hers. Pulling her close, he dipped his head. "Might as well give them a show."

His kiss had been hot before. Now it was so X-rated her body clenched in reaction. She pushed her hips against his fly and he gripped her tush, bringing her in even closer.

As he made love to her with his tongue and rocked his hips, her body responded. If he kept this up, if she didn't move away... she would....

With a soft cry of regret, she wiggled out of his arms and stepped back, panting. "Enough." She fumbled with the buttons of her coat.

"Yeah." Gulping for air, he shoved his hands in his jacket pockets, leaving his jacket open to the frigid air as he gazed up at the night sky. "To be continued."

"Oh?" She dragged in a breath. "Then you're not dumping me for my own good?"

He responded with a ragged chuckle. "I should, you know."

"But you can't, because I'm irresistible."

He leaned down and scooped up his hat. Then he met her gaze. "I've lived my whole life believing I can always walk away."

"Please don't walk away."

"That's the thing." He settled his hat on his head and buttoned his jacket. "For the first time ever, I'm not sure I can."

19

"We'd better go back." Cole had no interest in returning to the party, but the tempting alternative, leaving now with Mila, wouldn't be happening. He was the designated driver for Claudie, Rio and Monty. He made a point of honoring his commitments.

Maybe that was why he made so few of them. He'd been dangerously close to committing his future to Mila. Then reality had smacked him upside the head.

She deserved someone who could guarantee they wouldn't be a shitty father to her children. She needed a guy who looked forward to playing Santa for his kids on Christmas Eve.

Bile rose in his throat as his demons stirred. He was not that guy.

"Let's not go back just yet." Mila glanced toward the gazebo. "I'd like to check on the Angel Tree."

He pulled himself together. Better go along with her suggestion unless he was prepared to spill his guts. "Sure."

He'd been ignoring the gazebo with its large Christmas tree, Santa's elaborate chair and lighted garlands looped over each railing. Not surprising that the tree would have some sort of community charity attached to it. As he followed her up the steps, he braced himself for the hit.

The tree had been lovingly decorated with dozens of tiny white lights and what looked like handmade ornaments. A few white cardboard cutouts of angels were scattered among the lights and ornaments, with writing on each.

Oh, yeah, this wouldn't be fun.

"I love this tradition. It was my dad's idea years ago and ever since then the mayor's office has handled it." She started around the tree, reading each card. "I'm glad there aren't many angels left."

He knew the routine. The church his mother belonged to had something similar. Once he'd asked his mother if she'd put his and Jordie's names on angel cards so Santa would know what they wanted.

He'd been smacked for suggesting it. No kid of hers would ever ask for charity.

"Some folks are reluctant to let anyone know they're struggling, so Adam makes gentle inquiries and coaxes the parents to fill out cards for their kids."

"Good plan." He was impressed with himself. He sounded like a normal person.

"Folks deliver the gifts to his office and he takes them around on Christmas Eve."

"What if some cards don't get picked up?"

"On Monday Adam will buy those gifts and we'll all chip in to pay for them."

"What if something's sold out?"

"So far we've been lucky on that score." She peered more closely at one of the angels. "Aww, Benny Tredwell's dump truck is still here." She plucked it from the branch. "I saw a cool one in the General Store today. I'm buying him that."

"How about letting me do it?" Where had that insane idea come from? He needed another trip to the General Store like he needed a hole in the head.

The smile she gave him might've been one reason he'd made that suggestion. He'd gained points, something he still wanted even as he told himself this relationship was doomed.

"Awesome idea. Here you go." She handed him the angel tag. "Do you know the one I'm talking about? It was bright yellow and metal so it'll stand up to plenty of construction projects."

"I didn't see it, but it shouldn't be hard to find." And that was another reason those words had jumped out of his mouth. He'd wanted a dump truck for Christmas. Never happened.

He tucked the angel in his coat pocket. "What else have we got on here?" He reached for another angel. Clearly he was losing his ever-loving mind. Good thing the writing was large so he didn't need his glasses. "Clara wants Lego dinosaurs. I vaguely remember there used to be something like that."

"There's even more, now. I can get that."

"Or you can show me where they are."

"You want to go shopping again?" Her dark eyes sparkled.

"If you have the time."

"Technically I'm on vacation, but I can't speak for you."

"Barring an emergency, so am I. The front gate job is my last assignment until after Christmas."

"Then we should probably go to the General Store tomorrow to make sure we can still get stuff."

"Tomorrow's Sunday. They'll be—"

"They're open from ten to four. They always do that on the Sunday before Christmas for last-minute shoppers."

"Alrighty, then." He lifted another angel from a high branch. "Annie wants a...." He peered at the card. "What the fudge is a Mini Whinnies Barn Surprise?"

Mila laughed. "Little plastic horses you can play with. You don't know what breed or color you'll get until you open the box. Listen, I didn't bring you up here in hopes you'd grab a bunch of angel tags."

"But if we take them all, then Adam won't have to worry about it on Monday, right? And Monday's cutting it close for finding kids' toys." Even he knew that much.

"All that's true. If you and I pick up these things tomorrow, we can tell everyone the total when we get back."

"Not necessary. I'll handle it." He walked around the tree collecting the remaining cards. Tomorrow he might bitterly regret the impulse since it meant braving the General Store again.

But tonight all he could think about was making sure these kids got the toys they yearned for. And for reasons he didn't want to examine, he wanted to pay for them.

"That's very generous of you."

The warmth in her voice drew his attention. She was looking at him like she was ready to eat him up with a spoon. And he was more than willing to let her do it.

He needed her kisses like he needed oxygen, but once he got started he wouldn't be able to stop. "If we don't leave this gazebo and head back to the Raccoon in the next five seconds, I can't be responsible for my actions."

Her cheeks turned a pretty shade of rose. "Understood. Let's go." She headed down the steps.

He followed, careful not to touch her. "I don't think I should dance with you anymore tonight."

"I don't think you should, either. I'm even wondering if I should switch places with Claudie for the ride home."

"Please don't. I like having you up next to me."

"I like it, too. You look sexy when you're driving."

"So do you. I had to keep myself on a tight leash when you drove us into town today."

Her cheek dented in a smile. "Nice to know I'm not the only one."

"No, ma'am."

"We should take my truck again tomorrow. It's only fair since you volunteered tonight."

"Okay, I accept."

She glanced at him. "I really like that about you."

"What?"

"You don't have a macho need to always be in the driver's seat."

"You can thank Jordie for that." A sudden picture of her at three, fists propped on her hips as she defied him, made him grin. "She might be four years younger, but she let me know from the get-go that I wasn't the boss of her."

"I'll bet she did. That said, she idolizes you. And I think...." She took a breath. "Never mind. It's not my place."

"Hey." He caught her hand before they crossed the street. "I hope you know you can say anything to me. No rules."

She turned to him. "I could be wrong."

"So what? You could be right. What were you going to say?"

"Let me back up. I know for a fact Luis is happy about us being together. And I also think Jordan would like it to work out for us."

"No question."

"Really?"

"While we were out on the dance floor, she told me Luis was her saving grace. And you could be mine."

She looked startled. "Wow. That's...that's lovely."

"I tend to agree with her."

"You do? It didn't sound that way a while ago."

"You could be my saving grace, but it has to work both ways."

"Which it would. Claudie asked if you were *my guy*, meaning the one I've been waiting for. I didn't admit it to Claudie, but I knew you were my guy the day we met."

He swallowed. What a mess he'd gotten them into. "I felt the same. You know I do, but—"

"That's good enough for now." She gave his hand a squeeze. "Let's go back to the party."

20

Jordan had said Cole habitually short-changed himself and Mila was seeing it in real time. She'd just have to derail the tendency.

Fortunately for her cause, his body wasn't on board with that habit. Words weren't effective, but actions were. She could employ that strategy to its fullest once they were alone.

At the Raccoon's front door, he reached for the handle and paused. "Hang on. I meant to ask you this at the break, but then we went outside and I forgot." He glanced at her. "Would you consider singing with the band for the last set?"

"Me? I'm not a performer."

"But you sang with me at the wedding reception."

"That was different. It was just family and close friends."

"But you've sung in public before. I'd bet on it."

"Yeah, back in high school, in choir and a couple of musicals, but that's not like singing in a professional setting."

"But you could. You have the voice for it and Sam already said it's a great idea."

"You talked to him?"

"I did and he's all for it. You probably know the Christmas stuff they've been playing. And you said you'd help me with *Feliz Navidad.*"

"Well, sure, but—"

"I'd love to have you up there with me for the last set."

As if she could resist that comment or the eagerness in his smoke-gray eyes. Maybe she'd make a fool of herself, but at least she'd get to be with him. "Okay, we can give it a try."

"Excellent. I promise you'll have fun." He opened the door and ushered her inside.

The Rooty Toots welcomed her with such enthusiasm that she felt obligated to say she'd never sung professionally. She'd performed before an audience this large during the high school musicals, but they'd rehearsed the heck out of those numbers.

The band started her off with *Winter Wonderland.* Sam offered to harmonize if she'd take the melody. Nerves jangling, she agreed. What had Cole gotten her into?

But after the first few lyrics, her jitters disappeared and her love of singing took over. Harmonizing with Sam was easy and the mellow notes from Cole's fiddle blended in like a dream.

Partway through she flashed him a smile and he responded with a wink. Dancers whirled around the floor, moving to music she'd helped create. Yeah, she liked this. A lot.

The applause at the end felt damn good, too. At the reception she'd sung along with Cole's fiddle playing mostly to flirt with him. She'd chalked up his compliments to him flirting back.

But his suggestion tonight had nothing to do with flattery. Evidently he valued her talent and liked making music with her. Heady stuff.

For the next hour she summoned her inner Faith Hill, throwing herself into Christmas classics like *Jingle Bell Rock, Santa Baby* and *Sleigh Ride.* Although she harmonized each number with Sam, she remained acutely aware of that fiddle and the man who was playing it.

As midnight grew closer, she was about to remind Luis about Tia Ezzie's request when Sam announced a short break and approached her with more sheet music.

He held it out. "Cole said your auntie wants us to play *Feliz Navidad.*"

"She does, and I know it, so I don't need that."

"This is a little different, the duet version, and I was hoping—"

"The one with Michael Bublé and Thalia? I love that!" She took the sheet music. "I'd be honored to sing it with you."

"Great." He smiled. "I've had this tucked away, too, waiting for a Spanish-speaking vocalist to take her part."

"You found her. Give me a minute to show this to Cole so he'll be up to speed. He doesn't know the song."

"Sure."

Sheet music in hand, she approached Cole, who was chatting with Billy, the drummer.

He glanced up. "Did you say yes to the *Feliz Navidad* duet?"

"You bet I did. I thought you'd like to take a look at the music. Ever played the song?"

"No, ma'am. Billy says the original is really simple, but the duet adds quite a bit to it."

"Right." She grabbed the music stand they'd set aside and laid the sheet music on it just as Sam walked over.

He glanced at Cole. "I see you reaching for your glasses, but I don't think you need to see the sheet music. Ever improvise?"

Cole smiled. "All the time."

"Then don't worry about the melody. Just get a sense of it and jump in with some flourishes whenever you want."

"Sounds like fun."

"That's what I like to hear." He picked up the music stand. "C'mon, Mila, let's go impersonate Michael and Thalia."

When Sam announced what they were about to attempt, a ripple of excitement moved through the room. "You're welcome to join in on the chorus," he told the crowd before adjusting his guitar strap. "Ready Thalia?"

She grinned. "Ready, Michael. Start us off." If she hadn't been performing for almost an hour, she'd be scared stiff, but she'd become comfortable on this stage. On top of that, she'd sung Thalia's part a million times. Still, she kept the sheet music in front of her because it was a complicated duet.

And a romantic one, weaving a love song into the traditional Christmas greeting. Sam delivered the Spanish opening perfectly, his voice that of a tender lover pledging his heart to his beloved.

She barely had time to wonder if Sam had a sweetheart before it was time to join him in the song. Ah, how she wished Cole knew more Spanish so he'd understand what she was saying with those words.

Her family did, and when she peeked at them, the joy on their beloved faces, especially Tia Ezzie's, made her tear up. But she never lost her concentration, not even when Cole began to play, overlaying the melody with rich tones that emphasized the romantic words. Maybe he knew those words, after all.

Would the crowd join in? She hoped so. This song was made for that, for bringing everyone together in the spirit of the season.

Then she heard them, the Dazzling Damsels, singing for all they were worth. That was all it took and soon the room was vibrating with the heartfelt words — Feliz Navidad. How could Cole not love this outpouring of goodwill?

As the final notes of the song were followed by thunderous applause, she glanced over at him. He looked dazed, and maybe that was a good thing.

Sam decided to close out the set with *All I Want for Christmas Is You,* and insisted she perform it solo. Caught up in the moment, adrenaline pumping, she sang directly to Cole.

He responded by locking his gaze with hers during the entire number. As the last note died away and the applause began, he tipped his hat to her. None of that went unnoticed by her brothers, who added whistles of approval to the round of applause.

As for Cole, he chuckled and ducked his head. But then he glanced up and sent her a look so intense she quivered with longing.

The effect of that intimate moment remained with her as the party broke up and everyone headed outside. Cole took her hand, his fingers sliding through hers and tightening as they exited surrounded by the Bridger Bunch.

Her family kept up a steady flow of alcohol-induced banter, alternating between raving about hers and Cole's musical abilities and teasing them about the heat they'd generated onstage. The joking continued as Claudie, Monty and Rio piled into the backseat of Cole's silver truck and Cole helped her into the passenger seat.

"Is it me or is it hot in this truck?" Rio settled in and buckled up.

Mila turned and gave him a look.

Claudie giggled as Cole climbed behind the wheel. "For sure it's smokin' hot up front." Then she ducked her head and lowered her voice. "But maybe we shouldn't tease the guy who volunteered to haul our asses home."

Cole snorted. "Excellent point." He backed out of the parking space.

"Hey, Claudie-waddie, whatcha doin' in the middle?" Rio had definitely imbibed freely tonight. He hadn't used that nickname in years.

"I like it here."

"Aha!" Rio tapped Cole on the shoulder. "See? She likes sittin' in the middle."

"Glad to hear it." Cole winked at Mila.

That wink had more power every time he used it. The trip home would be a long one, especially with Claudie and Rio in the back laughing and whispering about them. Monty, as usual, was asleep.

"Hey, Claudie-waddie." Rio ducked his head, as if he thought that would muffle his voice. "See how they're lookin' at each other?"

She hunkered down, too. "They're in luuuv."

"Yeah, but I don't wanna end up in a ditch."

"Don't worry. I'm watchin' for funny business."

Mila glanced at Cole. "Please excuse them. They're plastered."

"No, really?"

"Am not," Claudie sang out.

"Me, either!" Rio used his hat to cover the space between the driver and passenger seat and went back to whispering. "Whatcha gonna do if there's funny business?"

"Poke 'em."

Grinning at Cole, Mila reached over and put a hand on his thigh. He returned the favor. The warmth of his hand was sweet torture since home was still almost thirty minutes away, but she couldn't resist trolling her siblings.

Rio moved his hat. "Uh-oh! Funny business!"

Mila lost it. She had to abandon the game to dig out a tissue from her tiny purse and mop the tears of laughter from her face.

"Hey, Claudie-waddie, you didn't poke 'em."

"Didn't have to. They stopped."

After blowing her nose, Mila turned to gaze at her sister and brother. "No poking."

Claudie gave her a Cheshire Cat grin. "Tell us the surprise and we won't bug you."

"Good one!" Rio bumped his shoulder against Claudie's. "Tell us and you can put your hands wherever you wanna."

"What if I wanna put them around your neck, *muchacho*?"

"You know what?" Cole put on his turn signal and pulled onto the two-lane highway. "Why not let them try to guess the surprise?"

"Seriously?"

"Sure. I'll throw out the first clue. The surprise is very sweet."

"That's a great clue." She was impressed. He might be better at playing these games than she'd expected.

"Cupcakes are sweet," Rio said.

"Cupcakes?" Claudie laughed. "It's been two months. He was buildin' somethin', like... like maybe—"

"Somethin' ta hold cupcakes! A Chrismus tree!" Rio sounded pleased with himself.

"For two months? He woulda finished in two days. It's not a cupcake tree."

"Maybe it's like...a... Chrismus tree made of... I dunno... *horseshoes*!"

"Come on, Rio. Ya don't weld horseshoes in the *hayloft*. You'd burn that sucker down."

Mila liked this bunny trail and didn't want them to abandon it. "What if he built something without welding?"

Cole nodded. "Polyurethane adhesive is a wonderful thing."

"What fits in a horseshoe?" Rio punched his hand in the air. "A cupcake!"

Claudie snorted. "It'd fall through and go plop, silly."

"What if he put another one facin' up? Or two facin' up?"

"Might work."

"Damn straight. Woo-hoo, guessed it! Horseshoe cupcake Chrismus tree. High five!"

"Hold on a dang minute. Does he bake?"

"I dunno." Rio tapped him on the shoulder again. "Do ya bake, dude?"

"Sometimes."

"See? It's a horseshoe cupcake Chrismus tree."

"Nosir. It's somethin' way cooler. And *I* live with Mila. She's gonna spill the beans."

"There's only one flaw in that logic." Mila turned toward the back seat. "I won't be spending much time with you between now and Christmas."

Her eyes widened. "You're movin' in with Cole?"

"I didn't mean that." The tantalizing prospect had occurred to her but it seemed a little soon. "We're taking it slow."

Rio chuckled. "Could've fooled me."

"Hmm." Claudie sank back against the seat. "Mila bakes."

"It's Mila's cupcakes in the horseshoes?"

"Could be. She's gonna add somethin' to it."

"Okay, then." Rio leaned forward. "Cupcake horseshoe Christmas tree. Are we right?"

Cole met Rio's gaze in the rearview mirror. "No."

"Well, fudge it all." He flopped back against the seat. "Fluffy fudge it all."

"*Fluffy?*" Claudie giggled. "Where did that come from?"

"My mouth. It came from my mouth."

"I know, dummy. But Cole says just plain fudge."

"I'm addin' my own twist and that's what came to me. Fluffy fudge it all."

"Tomorrow I'm gonna think that's stupid. Tonight it's sooo funny. Fluffy fudge it all! Maybe Cole hates it."

"I don't."

Claudie let out a deep sigh. "Good thing it's not a horseshoe cupcake Chrismus tree. It's somethin' better, right?"

Mila exchanged a look with Cole. "Way better."

He reached for her hand. "Thanks for that."

"Claudie-waddie. Check it out. Funny business."

"They're just holdin' hands and we're close to home. No biggie."

Easy for Claudie to say. She wasn't the one holding Cole's hand. They'd be parked by the barn in less than ten minutes.

Cole brushed his thumb over her palm in a lazy caress, sending her pulse into overdrive. She snuck a glance at him.

He sucked in a breath and turned his head. "Almost there."

"Yeah." *Oh, yeah.*

21

Cole switched off the engine and fought the urge to leap out and dash toward the stairs, Mila in tow. Instead he made sure everyone was headed in the right direction — Rio climbing the snowy hill to his A-frame, Monty ambling across the yard to his cottage near the main house and Claudie walking through the gate of the mini-hacienda she shared with Mila.

"They're all fine." Mila pulled on her gloves. "We can go."

He tugged on his gloves and took her hand. "How about I throw you over my shoulder and we go up the stairs that way?" Dumb idea, but he desperately wanted to save her the climb.

She laughed. "How about we skip that so you don't dislocate something in the process? Come on." She started off at a brisk pace. "The sooner we conquer those stairs the sooner we can—"

"Point taken. I used to think they were cool. Tonight they're a pain in the ass."

"Want to do it in the barn?"

"I'd be tempted if I had a condom in my pocket." He released her hand as she reached the base of the stairs. "Don't go too fast. I don't want you to slip."

"Backatcha. I don't want you to run me over."

"If I'm not careful, I might. Those last two miles were tough duty."

"But we made it." Gripping the railing, she continued upward, her boots slipping on the icy surface.

"Better slow down."

"Don't want to."

Much as he loved hearing that, if she fell and hurt herself, he'd never—

"Is your door unlocked?"

"Yes, ma'am."

"*Bueno.*"

"For future reference, it always is."

"Is that an invitation?"

"Absolutely." The air was so cold it made his eyelids hurt, but inside he was a furnace of desperation.

Gasping from effort and excitement, sending out puffs of condensed air like the little train in the storybook, he stayed right behind her. Almost there.

Two steps left. One step — and she stumbled, slamming into him.

"Ayiyi! Sorry!"

"I've gotcha." He'd almost gone down, but somehow he'd defied the law of physics, caught her and held on. His body served as a temporary barricade against what would be a devastating fall.

Unfortunately his boots had slid on impact and his heels hung out over thin air. He couldn't balance on the balls of his feet for long. If they tumbled the length of these metal stairs....

Good thing he'd ended up with his mouth conveniently next to her ear. "Get your feet under you."

"*Dios*, that feels sexy."

"Hurry up before we both head for the bottom."

"*Si, si.*" Grabbing the railing with both hands, she righted herself and planted her feet on the last step. "*Gracias, mi amor.*"

He dragged in a breath. "Hearing you say that was almost worth the terror of the moment."

"You were terrified?" She made it onto the landing and reached for the door. "You didn't sound terrified."

"My boots slipped when I caught you. We almost—"

"But you saved us." She clutched the front of his jacket and pulled him through the open door.

"Thank God." Shoving the door closed, he wrapped her in his arms, coat and all. "Thank God." He captured her mouth with no thought as to what was supposed to come next. He only knew he needed this kiss more than he needed air.

Clothes started coming off as they shuffled their way into the bedroom, but every time he momentarily lost contact with her mouth, he immediately reconnected. He kept kissing her even as he rolled on the condom he'd left lying within reach on the bedside table.

Finally, just before he sank his demanding cock into her sweet warmth, he lifted his head and gazed down at this woman he was privileged to have lying beneath him. "I'm so glad you're here."

The glow in her brown eyes softened and she cupped his face in both hands. "So am I, *mi amor*. So am I."

Leaning down, he kissed her again, gently this time as he lowered his hips and accepted the gift she offered. His heart stuttered as he pushed deeper.

The earthy scent of her arousal filled his nostrils. The sound of her rapid breathing was the only one that mattered.

His chest tingled as he surged forward and brushed over her taut nipples. Her arms tightened around him and her fingers pressed into his back.

As the tip of his cock touched her womb, he paused to absorb, the moment, the miracle of loving Mila. He shook with eagerness, yet homage must be paid to this blessing.

Then it began, his heart creating a drumbeat of celebration, of recognition, of certainty... *this is it, this is it, this is it*. He began to stroke in time with that rhythm. He slowly ended the kiss so he could look at her.

The truth was there, shining in her eyes, glowing on her cheeks. She felt it, too. They'd been given a once-in-a-lifetime chance. It was theirs to enjoy. Or destroy.

He didn't know which way it would go, but right now, making love to her, his world was sprinkled with stardust. Wrapped in her arms, joined with her in this intimate dance, he'd never been so sure that he was exactly where he was supposed to be.

As her body quickened beneath him, as her eyes and her breathing told him all he needed to know, he loved her instinctively, following her unspoken cues. She rose to meet him, slid her hands to his hips to urge him on.

Her gasps of pleasure and delight filled him with joy. When her cries became more urgent, he moved faster. They rode the whirlwind, spinning out of control together, laughing and shouting like kids on a rollercoaster.

Bliss.

Breathing hard and filled with gratitude, he gazed down at Mila. "I want to do this all night long."

"Me, too."

"You're not sleepy?"

"Not right now."

"Alrighty, then. See you in a few minutes." He left for the bathroom.

He was probably gone for all of five minutes, but when he came back, her eyes were closed and her breathing was shallow. When he murmured her name, she didn't stir.

As he started toward the bed, his bare foot came in contact with something on the floor and he glanced down. Her dress. Picking it up, he shook it out and laid it carefully over the chair in the corner. Then he located her undies and put them there, too.

Leaving his clothes on the floor, he climbed carefully into bed and pulled up the covers before snuggling in next to her. He'd had visions of turning on the fireplace and cuddling while they gazed at the dancing flames before they made love again.

Didn't matter. He had a hunch she'd spend tomorrow night here, maybe Monday and Tuesday night, too. As for Christmas Eve....

Could he manage Christmas Eve, too? Could the promise of another night in her arms block out his nightmare once and for all?

He wanted to believe that. Lying to her about his reason for skipping the festivities would be a betrayal. It could destroy the mutual trust they were building.

But finding the strength to celebrate Christmas Eve with Mila wouldn't be easy. It could be a turning point, though, a golden chance to bury his poisonous memories. Was he up to it? If he wanted a life with Mila, he'd damn well better be.

22

Mila woke up slowly, cautiously. She wasn't in her own bed, so where was she?

Oh. Cole lay facing her, sound asleep.

In the pale light filling the room, she studied his relaxed features — the arch of his eyebrows, the curve of his mouth and the shadow of his beard.

Amazingly soft, his close-trimmed beard added a roguish touch, especially when those talented lips were tilted in a cute little half-smile and he gave her a wink. She hadn't noticed his long lashes until now, when his eyes were closed.

They'd made love two nights in a row, and yet she hadn't really taken time to admire his solid physique in detail. But she remembered very well how his body felt.

She relived the sensation of his chest hair tickling her breasts as he moved, his gaze locked with hers. She remembered the tension, the tantalizing friction, the way he answered the deep ache within her, his sure strokes bringing her to a shattering climax.

Given the excellence of that experience, how in hell had she fallen asleep? If they spent the night together again, and she figured they would, she'd make sure to stay awake longer.

His lashes fluttered and he opened his eyes. His initial blink of surprise was followed by a glow of anticipation that grew stronger by the second.

She smiled. "Good morning."

He sucked in a breath. "If this is a dream I don't want to wake up."

"It's not a dream and I owe you an apology. After announcing I was ready to make love until dawn, I conked out. Some hot lover I am."

He slid his arm around her waist. "Yes, ma'am. Hottest lover ever."

"Nice of you to say, but—"

"You had a long day followed by a big party. You did an awesome job singing with the band, by the way."

"I loved it, loved being up there with you. I'm so glad you talked me into it, but I must have been more tired than I thought."

He smiled. "Obviously."

"But I swear, in that moment, I really did think I could go all night."

"How about in this moment?"

Color bloomed in her cheeks. "Hmm. Perhaps I can make it up to you for being such a party pooper." She reached under the covers.

He gasped as she wrapped her fingers around his cock. "Careful. It's loaded."

She reluctantly let go. She hadn't spent nearly enough time exploring the playground he offered. "Then how about rolling over and finding another one of those little raincoats for our friend?"

"Will do."

When he turned away and reached for the bedside table drawer, she flipped back the covers and sat up.

He glanced over his shoulder. "Got plans?"

"I do. Give me the condom and lie back."

He handed her the small package, stretched out and stuffed a pillow behind his head. "I'm beginning to understand what you meant by *good morning.*"

"It can be so much more than a greeting." Ripping open the packet, she straddled him and rolled on the condom. "It can be a promise."

"I can see that." His words were casual, but the huskiness in his voice and the gleam in his eyes gave him away.

Her body thrummed with urgency, but she kept her hips elevated as she flattened her palms against his broad chest. Leaning down, she kissed him gently. Then she pushed up and gazed into his eyes. "*Buenos dias*, Cole."

The gleam in his eyes intensified. "*Buenos dias*, Mila."

Gradually she lowered her hips, swiveling them, brushing the tip of his cock, teasing him a little before she zeroed in.

His breathing roughened. "You know I want to grab you and get this party started."

"But you won't."

"This is your show."

"Do you like having me take charge?"

His chest heaved. "Very much."

"Good. So do I." Heart thumping, she settled into position, just barely making the connection. "Having fun?"

He gulped for air. "Fudge, yeah."

She eased down a little more. "I have a question."

"Okay."

"When you soundproofed this place..." She took him a little deeper.

He gasped. "What about it?"

"Did you think of this?" She thrust downward, taking him up to the hilt.

He groaned. "Yes."

"Was I part of that decision?"

"Always." He held her gaze. "I knew—" He dragged in a breath. "If it ever happened, we'd be loud."

She chuckled. "You were right." He'd created this loft with her in mind. Knowing that made her giddy. And a bit wild. "Let's test the limits." Tightening her core, she began to pump. Sure enough, his low moans grew in volume.

She picked up speed, panting with the effort as his moans became cries that turned to straight out yelling. Success.

"Now!" Grasping her hips, he held her in place as he pushed upward. The strong pulsing of his cock sent her over the edge. Tossed in the rolling seas of a powerful climax, she added her hoarse shouts to his as the waves crashed against her trembling body.

The celebration deep in her core slowly grew quiet as she sucked in air. Cole looked as dazed as she felt. "How're you doin', cowboy?"

He swallowed. "This is the best morning of my life."

"Yeah?"

"Yeah. No contest." He met her gaze as he caressed her hips and slid his hands up her back. "Thank you."

"I had a good time, too."

He smiled. "I could tell. What does *que alegria* mean?"

"I said that?"

"A couple of times."

"It means *what joy.*"

"What joy, indeed." He stroked her back. "I have an idea. Let's go saddle up Sparky and Sol."

"Now?"

"If we hurry, we'll have them back before feeding time. We can take carrots as an appetizer. I'm talking about a short ride to watch the sunrise." His face was alight, like a kid's on Christmas morning.

"Great idea, but I don't have the right clothes."

"Oh." The eagerness in his eyes faded. "Of course you don't. I didn't think of—"

"I just need ten minutes." She wanted to bring back that happy expression she'd squelched. "I'll run home and be back before you know it." She eased away from him. "I'll meet you in the barn."

Grasping the condom, he sat up. "Are you sure? It's not too much trouble?"

"It's no trouble." She noticed that her clothes, which she'd left on the floor, were neatly laid on an armchair in the corner. "Thanks for picking up my things." She quickly pulled on her underwear.

"You bet." He headed for the bathroom. "While you get changed, I'll tack up the horses."

"Alrighty." She pulled her dress over her head and carried her boots out to the living room. "Don't forget the carrots!" she called out as she put on her boots and picked up her coat from the living room floor. "We'll need to bribe those horses to leave the cozy barn!"

"I know! Watch your step on the stairs!"

"Absolutely!" She hurried out the door but exercised care on those steps. The cold air was a shock that took her breath away, but her body hummed with heat and energy.

Claudie had left the front gate open and chances were good she was still dead to the world. Nevertheless, stealth was called for to make sure she didn't wake up and slow the process.

After changing into jeans, a sweater and her riding boots, Mila grabbed a few clothes and threw them into a duffle along with her basic toiletries on the assumption she'd stay at Cole's tonight, too. She wasn't moving in, but it would be nice to have some of her stuff.

Then she was out the door again, wearing her red parka with the hood down because she'd put on her Stetson. She'd shoved her truck keys in the pocket for the trip to town later on.

Walking around to the front of the barn, she found Sparky and Sol tied to the hitching post. Sol was saddled and ready to go.

Cole appeared carrying Sparky's blanket, saddle and bridle. "Wow, you're fast!"

"Gotta beat the sun."

"We will." He carried the tack over to the hitching post. "Whatcha got in the duffle?"

"Just a few things. Don't worry. I'm not moving in."

He glanced over his shoulder. "Who says that would worry me?"

"It wouldn't?"

"Are you kidding? After what happened this morning?"

She laughed. "Don't go thinking that would be a regular occurrence."

"A guy can hope." He flashed her a grin. "How about sticking the duffle in the tack room for now?"

"My thoughts exactly. The stairs take time."

"The stairs need an overhaul. It was fine when I was the only one going up and down, but now...."

"We can toss around ideas on the ride." She hurried into the barn and stowed her duffle in a corner. The horses were stomping and talking among themselves, stirred up because two humans had arrived but no food had been delivered.

"Breakfast will be served soon, guys and gals." Her reassurance brought a few nickers and a couple of snorts. "Most likely Adam and Tracy or Luis and Jordan." For sure it wouldn't be Rio, Monty or Claudie. Or Zay. He'd thoroughly enjoyed himself last night, too.

When she walked out of the barn, Cole stood waiting, a hand on the bridle of each of their horses. "Thanks for indulging me."

"Thanks for getting them ready. It'll be fun. We've never taken a ride together." Clutching a handful of Sol's cream-colored mane, she placed her foot in the stirrup and swung into the saddle.

"I never dared ask." He mounted up. "Thought it might be too pointed, too much like a date."

"We skipped right over that phase."

"Never liked it much, anyway." He turned Sparky toward the path between the barn and the pasture.

She followed him to the electronic gate just beyond the barn and waited while he tapped in the code. On their left, the Flint Creek Range lay in shadow, backlit by the glow of the sun that hadn't yet peeked over the snowy peaks.

She had a hunch where he was headed, and it wasn't far.

He nudged Sparky into a slow canter, ducking under low branches as he led the way down a narrow trail through the pines. It hadn't snowed in a couple of weeks and the path was clear, but snow still clung to patches in the forest that never saw sunlight.

About a mile down the trail, he took a fainter path that veered off to the left. A few yards later, the pines gave way to a meadow and a view of the mountains.

He pulled Sparky to a halt. "I found this spot weeks ago one morning when I wanted a good place to watch the sun come up. You probably knew where we were going."

"I did. Great place to watch the sunrise. I used to do it a lot, but then we got busy."

"I haven't been out here much, either." He glanced at her. "But I'm always glad when I make the effort."

"I know what you mean. You watch the sun come up, and you hear the song from *Annie* in your head."

He laughed. "Can't say that I do."

"But now you will. You're welcome for the earworm."

"I was about to get philosophical."

"*Annie* is very philosophical. It's about triumphing over adversity and beginning a new chapter."

"Then I guess that song is appropriate." He rested his gloved hands on the saddle horn and watched as the jagged edge of the peak began to glitter as if being painted in gold leaf by an invisible brush.

She appreciated the beauty of the scene, but she was more captivated by the image of Cole in profile, astride that magnificent chestnut horse, gazing at the mountains... and into the future. "I love that you suggested this."

He turned to her. "You don't think it's corny?"

"No. It's perfect." Taking off her right glove, she held out her hand. Taking off his left glove, he laced his fingers through hers and looked into her eyes as the sun crested the ridge, bathing them in golden light.

23

Mila had insisted that she wasn't moving in, but it felt like it and Cole had no objection whatsoever. He'd never lived with a girlfriend, never cared to. But Mila brought energy into his space that he hadn't even known was missing.

Sharing an apartment with Jordie had told him a lot about co-existing with a woman. She'd taught him to value a scrubbed bathroom and a neat kitchen. He was used to putting down the toilet seat and picking up his clothes.

But living with Jordie hadn't prepared him for the thrill of having Mila in residence. He'd imagined her living with him — likely why he'd created a shower big enough for two. She'd been his inspiration for hauling a king-sized bedframe up to the loft and hanging a dramatic electric fireplace within view of that bed.

After the ride they'd made love again and showered together. If they hadn't been starving, they would have ended up back in bed. Instead they'd dressed and made breakfast in a kitchen with enough counter space to work side-by-side. His choices during the renovation made sense at last.

Only one silly little thing sat like a very small burr under his saddle of happiness. While they'd dressed after their shower, she'd balked at his suggestion to unpack her duffle and put her clothes in his dresser and/or his closet.

As they sat eating breakfast, her duffle was visible beside the armchair near the open barn doors. She'd moved her toothbrush, lotions and makeup into the bathroom, so why not unpack her clothes? It bugged him.

He should let it go. It wasn't important.

"I'll bet I know what you're thinking."

"Is that so?" He glanced at her.

"You keep looking at my duffle and wondering why I didn't unpack it."

"Good guess."

"I'd thought I might, but while we were getting dressed, I read a text Claudie had sent earlier. That reminded me that I can only stay here tonight and tomorrow night. That should give me plenty of time to make the Santa hats. Then I'll need to go home."

"Because of Claudie?"

She gazed at him as if considering how to answer.

"I know you like it here."

"I do, and I'm not saying I won't come back after Christmas. That's if you want me to."

That sounded a long time away. "You know I do. Are you worried that we're moving too fast? Do you need a break from me?"

"That's not it." She sighed. "Look, it's obvious Christmas isn't important to you, and I would never want you to fake it for my sake. It's fine that you don't care about decorations and trees and listening to Mannheim Steamroller, but I do."

"Who's Mannheim Steamroller?"

"You just made my point. Their Christmas albums are really popular. They go on tour every year and I got to see them once in Missoula. That concert was the highlight of my Christmas."

"Now that you mention the tour, I might have heard of them, after all." Chances were good his parents hadn't played their music so he'd probably be okay with it. "If you want to put it on while you're here, that's okay with me."

"That's sweet of you but being okay with it isn't the same as loving it. Claudie and I love it. We blast it through the house when we make our Christmas fudge."

"Fudge? Really?"

"Yeah, I know. It's your special word, but it's also our thing we do. We make up tins of it to give to everybody. You'll get one, unless you don't like fudge, which would be ironic."

"I'd love to have some of your homemade fudge." He was beginning to get the picture. He could ask if she'd consider spending the night with him after she'd made fudge with Claudie while blasting Mannheim Steamroller.

But that would reveal his neediness, and he wasn't prepared to do that. She also might turn down his offer.

It wasn't just the fudge project. She didn't want to spend the two days before Christmas with the Grinch in his cave, which had only a small tree that he'd yet to plug in, let alone find a place for.

"Cole." She reached over and took his hand. "It's only a couple of days."

He glanced up. "I'm just sorry I'm not enthusiastic about something you enjoy."

"I gather your folks weren't big into it."

"Not really."

"Was it a religious thing?"

"No. It was... we didn't have much money and so... it made them angry more than anything."

"I can imagine that happening."

Could she? A person who'd never experienced poverty?

Maybe she could see the doubt in his expression, because she quickly added to her comment. "I mean, sort of. I was lucky to end up in this family and I know it." She hesitated. "What about Jordan?"

"She's doing okay. She knows how much Luis cares about this holiday and now their baby news has added a special glow to everything. She'll be fine."

"You cushioned her from some of the disappointment, didn't you?"

His breath caught. "I'm not sure what you—"

"Hey, I'm the oldest, too. I was four when my biological dad died. I remember it and I remember worrying about how Luis and Zay were taking everything. When we came here I was like a mother hen. If Luis and Adam got into it, I was the one who broke up the fight until Luis begged me to stop babying him."

"Yeah, Jordie told me to stop worrying about her, too. Said she could take care of herself, but I kept a watch on her, anyway."

"You still do."

"I guess."

"So do I, although now that Luis has Jordan, I'm not really worried anymore."

"Same here. Jordie's gonna have a great life with Luis. He's a good guy."

"The best." She let a moment of silence pass. "What I'm trying to say in a roundabout way, is that I get that Christmas doesn't work for you, at least now. You may eventually change your mind, but I would never expect you to force yourself into anything or pretend to like it."

"I appreciate that."

"So I'll go do my thing and we can pick up where we left off after it's over."

"All right." But the upshot was he wouldn't have her around in the two days leading up to Christmas Eve. He'd been unconsciously counting on that to help desensitize him.

"I do hope you'll come to the family dinner on Christmas Eve, though."

"You have a family dinner?" Anxiety curled in his stomach.

"We do. Then after the meal we walk down to the barn, assuming there's not a blizzard. Oh, and we sing carols. We sing on the way down and keep it up when we go into the barn to give treats to the horses."

"Fun." Could he manage that? It was whacky enough that he might be able to, assuming he didn't lose ground during her absence.

"It'll be Sparky's first Christmas, so he won't know the routine, but the other ones do. When they hear us singing, they get excited. Treats and all that attention. They love it."

"I'll bet they do."

"On this same topic, we should get going if we want to avoid the midday rush at the General Store." She squeezed his hand and let go. "We… oh, wait. You don't have to go."

"But I want to."

"Do you?" She met his gaze. "Now that I know more about your childhood, I'm thinking it wasn't a bad hard-boiled egg and moldy bagel that upset your system yesterday."

He sighed. "No, it wasn't, and I should have leveled with you. I'm sorry."

"Listen, no worries. I'll pick up those things."

Did he want to go? No. Was he going anyway? Damn right he was. "It's a good cause, one I believe in. I'll enjoy picking out gifts for those kids." He really wanted to believe that.

Her response was a smile with enough wattage to power a guy through a dozen Christmas shopping trips. "Okay, then, *mi amor. Vamanos!*"

24

"Not many vehicles on the Square yet."

"Give it another hour and it'll be packed." Mila parked in front of the General Store. More informed than she'd been during yesterday's shopping gig, she picked up on the stiffness in Cole's posture. But in her estimation, he'd made the right choice.

"Probably be really crowded next year if Adam's beloved road is finished." He made no move to unlatch his seatbelt.

She took her cue from him and stayed put. "Yeah, I was sad for him that they didn't get 'er done by fall."

"But the Rowdy Ranch crew came to the wedding anyway."

"They did. I know the road will be good for the town's economy. But selfishly I want it done so the McLintocks have a shortcut and we'll see them more often."

"I predict it'll be done by sometime in June."

"I hope so. They'll want to come see that baby, for sure."

"They will."Taking a breath, he reached for his seatbelt. "Let's go see what we can find." Although he flashed her a smile, the haunted look in his eyes told a different story.

Mentally crossing her fingers, she climbed out and crossed the sidewalk with him to the store's entrance just as Polly, one of the clerks, unlocked the door.

"Come in, come in! Goodness you're the early birds, aren'tcha? Hi, Mila. It's Cole, right?"

"Yes, ma'am." He tipped his hat.

"Well, the store's all yours, at least for now. What's on the shelves is what we've got. Nothing left in the back."

"Good to know," Mila said. "Thanks, Polly."

"Need any help finding anything?"

Mila glanced at Cole. "Do we?"

"I think we've got it, but we'll holler if we need you, Polly."

"You do that. I'm by myself for now, so I have a few little chores to handle, if you'll excuse me. Have fun." She hurried toward the back of the store.

Cole pulled a shopping cart from the ones horizontally stacked by the entrance and then discarded it because it had a wonky wheel. The next one passed inspection. "Lead the way. Let's start with the dump truck."

"Good call." She headed for the toy section. Polly hadn't turned on the sound system yet and the silence felt weird, but if Cole was freaked out maybe it was just as well. "The shelves are definitely bare compared to yesterday."

"I'll take your word for it." He followed behind her.

He hadn't been paying attention at all? That surprised her. What she'd pegged as a disinterest in the holiday scene looked more and more like a phobia. What the hell had happened to him?

Luis had mentioned that Jordan didn't exactly love Christmas but she was being a good sport about it. At last night's party, Cole had seemed to enjoy himself, so she'd assumed he was being a good sport, too.

But he'd flinched when she'd mentioned the Christmas Eve dinner. She'd decided against calling attention to that. "Yay! There's the truck!"

"Only one left."

"Good thing we came early." She handed it to him. "You can check it over for defects, but if it's the last one...."

"I don't notice any nicks or dents." He turned the see-through package around almost lovingly as he examined it. "It's a good-looking truck. Benny's gonna love it."

Just like Cole would have when he was a kid. If he'd had one, he would have said so. The image of him as a disappointed little boy made her chest hurt. "If you want to ride along with Adam on Wednesday afternoon when he delivers the gifts, I'm sure he—"

"Thanks, but I'd rather not." He put the truck in the cart. "Where're the Mini Whinnies?"

"Around the corner. I used to practically live in that part of the store when I was little." She zipped around the endcap and plucked a box from the shelf. "Here you go."

He took it and frowned. "That's not very big."

"That's why they're called Mini Whinnies. It's what Annie asked for, so she knows the box is small."

He checked the price. "We should get her two."

"Okay." Much more of this and she'd be in tears over the tender-hearted kid living in this big cowboy's body. She handed him a second box.

"Jordie would have loved these. When did they first come out?"

"About twenty years ago."

"I must've missed them. If I'd seen them, I would've...." He shook his head. "Never mind. Where's the Lego dinosaur section?"

"Down here." She walked to the end of the aisle. "This is all the Lego stuff."

He scanned the shelves. "Wow. Clara didn't say which dinosaur. What if we get the wrong one?"

So vulnerable. Little did he know he was turning her into a puddle of goo. "I'm guessing she doesn't have any, so she'll be thrilled with whichever one you choose."

"There's everything from a T-Rex to a cute baby dinosaur. You were a little girl. What would you have picked?"

"None. I was into horses. But if she's into dinosaurs and doesn't have any, I'd get her the T-Rex. She can show it off because everyone will know immediately what it is and be impressed."

"Smart. I hadn't thought about the fact that she'll want bragging rights."

No bragging rights for little Cole. His childhood must have been bleak, and yet somewhere along the way he'd learned to play the violin.

Desperate to focus on something positive in his background, she brought it up. "When did you get your fiddle?"

"Not long after I moved out. It was at the second-hand shop where I bought things for my apartment. I paid for it over time. It belonged to the guy who owned the shop and he taught me to read music."

"Bonus. What made you want a fiddle?"

He smiled. "I heard *The Devil Went Down to Georgia* and became a huge Charlie Daniels fan."

"Then you can play that song?"

'Yes, ma'am."

"That number is a real crowd pleaser. How come you didn't play it at the wedding reception?"

"Wasn't appropriate, at least in my opinion. It's a performance number that puts the spotlight on the fiddler. That was Jordie and Luis's day, not mine, and the mood was all about romance, not a contest with the Devil."

Naturally he wouldn't want to steal the limelight from his little sis. She should have known. "Then promise me you'll play it at the New Year's Eve Party at the Raccoon."

He smiled for the first time since they'd walked through the door. "Only if Sam agrees to it and you'll be my date that night."

"I guarantee Sam will agree to it and I'd be honored to be your date."

"Excellent. Now let's get this shopping done before the place fills up and the selection dwindles." He pulled another angel card out of his coat pocket. "Dustin's a kid after my own heart. He wants Lincoln Logs. Do they still exist?"

"Over here." She moved to the opposite aisle, encouraged by the uptick in his mood. "Pricey, though."

"I don't care. I—" The sound system blared, cutting him off with *It's Beginning to Look a Lot Like Christmas.*

The volume was immediately turned down, but it was still loud and echoed in the empty store. It creeped her out and she wasn't the one with the problem.

The haunted look was back in Cole's eyes. A muscle twitched in his jaw as he put the Lincoln Logs in the cart and took out another angel card.

Clearly he'd been triggered by that song. She liked to give everyone the benefit of the doubt. Usually. But she had zero tolerance for adults who were mean to children.

If this relationship blossomed into something permanent, she might end up having to meet his parents. Could she even be civil? Doubtful.

Because this shopping trip was important to him and to the kids, she threw herself into the process, pumping it with all the enthusiasm she could muster. They managed to find everything. Thank goodness they'd only had eleven angel cards to deal with.

She made conversation with Polly as they checked out. Cole murmured his thanks and tipped his hat again before picking up both bags and carrying them out to the truck. The parking spots on the square were mostly taken by now, so if he wanted to stay for any reason, she might as well keep this space.

After they'd put the bags in the back seat, she turned to him. "Anything else you'd like to do while we're in town?"

He sighed in obvious relief. "Not me. I'm ready to—" Then he caught himself. "How about I treat you to lunch again?"

"How about we go home and have peanut butter and jelly?"

He nudged back his hat and gazed at her. Like the sun coming out from behind a cloud, his harried expression was replaced by a soft smile. "You're incredible."

"I'm glad you think so."

"You know I want to head home."

"And that's fine with me."

"I can tell, which is very sweet of you. And we definitely would end up eating peanut butter and jelly for lunch."

"Why not? It's everybody's favorite!"

"But then we'd be out of bread, which means we can't even make toasted cheese sandwiches for dinner."

"Doesn't matter. I can grab some food from my house."

"That's a generous offer, but instead we're going grocery shopping."

"They'll be playing Christmas music in there, too."

"I'm used to it. If I hadn't learned to tune it out while I bought groceries every December, I would have starved to death long ago." He held out his hand. "Let's go get us some grub."

"Grub." She took his hand and they walked across the square to the town's cozy food market. "My dad used to call it that."

"I heard it in a song by Ray Scott and liked the sound of it. Makes me feel like an old-timey cowboy."

"You are an old-timey cowboy."

"Am I?"

"Sure. I think of them as respectful, kind, modest, protective of those smaller or weaker. You fit the profile."

"That's a huge compliment. But as my behavior in the General Store shows, I'm also a work in progress."

"We all are."

"I'll have to disagree with you there. You're fudging perfect. Don't change a thing."

She laughed. "I'm not perfect. Just ask Claudie."

"She's welcome to her opinion. I'm sticking with mine."

"You're crazy."

"About you."

"You're not so bad, yourself, cowboy." Ah, this was more like it. He'd shaken off whatever ghosts had been summoned by that music in the General Store.

He'd had a tough childhood, no doubt about it. But now he was surrounded by the Bridger Bunch. It might take time, but he'd be okay. She'd see to it.

25

When it came to grocery shopping during the Christmas season, Cole had become so good at ignoring the music and decorations that he'd already navigated the Mustang Valley Market several times this month without breaking a sweat.

But he'd never enjoyed the process of buying food for himself regardless of the time of year. Having Mila along dramatically changed the program for the better.

He ended up checking out with a cart full of colorful veggies he never would have bought on his own — carrots maybe, but red beets, broccoli and sweet potatoes? Not at all. Her excitement about the fresh produce aisle was irresistible.

She'd clearly decided his diet needed an upgrade from chips, burgers and beer to healthier options. He couldn't disagree. If that upgrade included her presence in his kitchen, he was all for it.

She was still focused on the topic as they loaded the groceries in her truck and headed for the ranch.

"I can't believe you don't eat sweet potatoes." She said it as if he was missing out on the treat of a lifetime.

He shrugged. "Between the tedious job of cooking and mashing the potatoes and trying not to burn the marshmallow topping, they're too fussy for me."

"Which is why we're going to bake them and top them with sour cream."

"Sour cream? On sweet potatoes?"

"You've never tried it?"

"No, ma'am. I've only had them mashed and baked with marshmallows."

"Trust me, you'll love the savory and sweet combo."

"Okay." How easily she said that simple phrase. *Trust me.* And how quickly he'd agreed to trust her... on the sweet potato issue. And on most things, really. But not on everything.

Hard to do when he couldn't even trust himself. He'd failed to hold it together in the General Store. She hadn't mentioned it, likely because she didn't want to dig into it. Who would?

But now Christmas Eve loomed on the horizon like the thunderheads currently moving in from the west.

"I also like topping sweet potatoes with a cheese sauce, but that's more work." Mila flipped up the visor as the sun disappeared behind a bank of clouds. "I've been too busy to check the weather. This must be the snow they said might come in."

"Let me look." He consulted the weather app on his phone. "Seventy-five percent chance starting at six tonight."

"How much?"

"Ten to twelve inches."

"Not too bad. If we're lucky, it'll snow tonight and then clear off for the rest of the week."

"Hope so."

"We've had to skip our barn caroling routine three times that I can remember. It's not like it ruins Christmas Eve, but it's not the same if we can't do it. I'd really like you to go with us."

"I'd like that, too." Absolutely true, but only if he could convince himself he'd handle it well. "What do you sing?"

"We don't sing *It's Beginning to Look a Lot Like Christmas* if that's what you're wondering."

"Good." He appreciated the subtle acknowledgment minus any probing questions.

"Usually it's *Silent Night* or maybe *O Little Town of Bethlehem.* Or both, depending on how fast we walk. Could you handle those?"

"I like the idea of walking down and singing to the horses, so yeah, I'll probably be fine."

"Maybe you can replace bad memories with good ones." She glanced over at him as if seeking buy-in for her theory.

"That would be great." Yeah, this was a good track to run on.

"Did you enjoy the Christmas party? I know the baby announcement threw you for a loop, but you seemed fine with the music."

"I mostly concentrated on you."

"All the time?"

"Pretty much."

"Even when you played *Carol of the Bells*?"

"Especially then. That was all for you. Sam was being so considerate about providing the sheet music that I didn't have the heart to tell him I didn't need it for that number."

"I thought you didn't know any Christmas carols."

"In my mind, it's not a Christmas carol. The guy who sold me the fiddle gave me sheet music for it that was more than a hundred years old. It's a Ukrainian folk song about the New Year. They still perform it at New Year's festivities."

"No kidding. I've never heard that." She took a breath. "What did you think of *Feliz Navidad?*"

"I liked it. Got a little jealous of Sam, singing something with you that sounded romantic, even if I couldn't understand the words."

Her cheeks turned rosy. "It is romantic, two people expressing their love for each other."

"So I was right to be jealous of Sam." Those feelings had startled him. He wasn't the possessive type.

"Not if you consider that I thought of you the whole time, especially when you added those beautiful touches to the melody."

"Just trying to impress you."

"You impressed the whole roomful of folks. Did you like it when they joined in?"

Emotion swept through him, just as it had when the entire place erupted in song. "It was… not a feeling I'm used to, like I'm caught up in a wave."

"Could it be the Christmas spirit?"

"No." He didn't believe in such a thing, but it would be obnoxious to say it out loud. "I didn't hate it. The loud singing didn't affect me the way the music did in the General Store."

"I'm afraid I wasn't much help in there. Christmas music in an empty store felt weird to me, too. I didn't know what to do."

"Nothing you could do. I just had to work through it. I'm glad I was mostly okay at the Raccoon last night. I've loved that place ever since I walked in back in July. I guess it's so amazing that even Christmas can't ruin it for me."

She was quiet for a while after that. Then she cleared her throat. "Do you... do you want to tell me about—"

"No, I don't." Damn. She'd asked, after all.

"But maybe if you—"

"I have no interest in dredging it up. Your idea of making new memories to replace the old ones is a better way to go. I was hoping I could do that with buying the gifts this morning."

"You almost did."

"Almost. Next December I'll browse in the General Store several times until I've desensitized myself like I have with the market."

"That doesn't sound like fun."

"But it works. You saw I was totally fine while we bought groceries."

"You blocked out the music and the decorations at the market?"

"I always do. You made it even easier. Watching you get orgasmic over the red beets with the greens still attached was the best grocery shopping experience of my life."

"That's not quite what I meant by replacing bad memories with good ones. If I'm hearing you right, your method is to focus on only part of the experience and shut out anything that reminds you of Christmas."

"That's the gist of it. Obviously I can't always do it. I was fine until that music blasted. Pretty hard to ignore that many decibels, especially when I'm in a store that reminds me of—" Whoa, he'd almost gone there.

"Reminds you of what? I wish you'd—"

"It's better for me if I don't. It's no good dwelling on those things." He used to worry that Jordie remembered the scene in the Helena department store, but she'd only been fifteen months old. She'd never mentioned it, so obviously she'd been too young for it to make an impression.

"I can understand why you'd say that, but to me there's a problem with that strategy."

"Like what?"

"If you desensitize yourself to everything that represents Christmas, how will you ever learn to enjoy it?"

"I probably won't, but at least I can function."

"That makes me so sad."

Great. Now she felt sorry for him. "Think of me as someone from a different culture that doesn't celebrate this holiday. You grew up with Christmas as a positive so you can't imagine not having that joy. I didn't experience it the way you did, so I won't miss what I never had."

"I'm trying to understand, but...."

"Mila, you make me so happy that I don't need to feel Christmas joy. Honestly, I don't."

She let out a breath. "Do you think that's what Jordan's doing? Desensitizing herself so she can make Luis happy?"

"I doubt that's the case. I'm guessing she'll be able to gradually discover what the rest of you appreciate about this season."

"Then why isn't that possible for you?"

"Jordie's and my situations were different."

"Sounds like whatever went on, you took the brunt of it."

He didn't answer. They were getting into the weeds, and there were things he never wanted her to know, never wanted anyone to know.

"Your silence tells me that's true."

This would be a good time to lie to her, which had been his response to every woman he'd allowed himself to get close to. For whatever reason, he couldn't lie to Mila.

But he wouldn't spill his guts, either. Refusing to do that likely meant their relationship had an expiration date, just as he'd feared last night when they'd bumped up against the baby issue.

They weren't far from the ranch. Soon they'd be back in his loft with groceries that would take them through the next couple of days. And nights. His body warmed and his jeans grew tight.

Did he have the strength to give her up now, which was the sensible thing to do? He'd have to be the one. He couldn't picture her seeing the light and walking away.

She made the turn onto the ranch road, pulled up to the keypad and rolled down her window so she could punch in the code. The big gate swung open perfectly. "Nice job on the gate."

"Thanks."

She rolled up the window and drove through. "Are we back to you thinking we have no future?"

"I should have anticipated this would be a problem the minute you climbed the stairs with that little Christmas tree."

"I'll take it back to my house."

"That won't solve anything. Bottom line, you deserve someone who's excited about babies and Christmas. That's not me and we both know it. If we admit that now, we'll cut our losses."

"Then you want me to drop you and your groceries by the stairs and leave you there?"

"It's the smart way to play it."

"What about the Santa hats? Oh, wait, you probably hate that idea, anyway."

"No, I don't. I did at first, but then I saw them on the raccoons and they look cute as hell."

"See? You like *something* about Christmas. It's a start."

He groaned. "You're relentless."

"I believe in you."

"That's a mistake." His smartass comeback was automatic but those four words burrowed into his soul. *I believe in you.* Jordie was the only other person who'd told him that.

She paused by the second gate and repeated the keypad routine.

"If it's a mistake, you're gonna have to prove it to me, cowboy."

"I'm sure I will."

She drove up next to the steps. "That sounds suspiciously like you're caving."

"I should have my head examined."

"I'm more interested in examining other parts of you." She turned off the engine and glanced at him. "Shall we haul the groceries upstairs and see what happens?"

He met her gaze and anticipation sizzled in his veins. "Leave the fudging groceries."

<u>26</u>

Mila hopped out of the truck and ran toward the tall metal stairway. The sun had melted the ice so she didn't have to worry about slipping this time as she pounded up the steps. Cole was right on her heels.

He was convinced they had no future, but every time they made love, their bond grew stronger. Couldn't he feel that, too? She had to believe he did. Nothing else explained the urgency of his touch, the hunger in his eyes, the passion in his voice.

Wrenching open the door, she toed off her boots and kept going, tossing her coat on the kitchen island, whipping her sweater over her head and throwing it in the direction of the couch. As she dashed through the open barn doors into the bedroom, she put her hands behind her back and unhooked her bra.

Then she spun around and dropped it to the floor just as he barreled into the bedroom, his shirt hanging open, his chest heaving as he unfastened his jeans.

He closed the gap between them. "I need to touch you." Cupping her breasts, he leaned down to kiss her, his breath warm against her lips. "I fudging need *you*." He captured her mouth with a groan, as if they'd been separated for weeks. He grasped the yielding fullness of her breasts as if he'd never let go.

She clutched his head and gave as good as she got, holding nothing back, until he gasped and lifted his mouth from hers. His words came fast as he struggled for breath. "I'm gonna explode any second."

"Then we'd better—"

"Yeah."

He stepped away and they both stripped down. Throwing back the covers, she climbed in, shivering as her hot skin met cool sheets. Then she glanced up.

Cole stood beside the bed swearing softly as he fumbled with the condom, almost dropping it. "This is what you do to me."

"This is what we do to each other." She held out her arms. "And it's a good thing."

"I'd love to believe that." He came to her, nestling his hips between her thighs and bracing his weight on his forearms, but holding back. "I've never needed anyone this much."

"Me, either. When you said we should leave the groceries, I was ready to do it in the back seat."

The corners of his mouth tilted. "But it was full of groceries."

"Exactly." She gripped his firm butt. "Enough with the small talk."

"Yes, ma'am." Easing his cock partway in, he paused. "This won't change anything."

"Wanna bet?" She lifted her hips, taking him deeper.

"No." He sucked in a breath. "I want to make love until we can't see straight." Holding her gaze, he pushed deep and began to stroke.

Nothing fancy. No candlelight. No music. No scented oils. Yet in seconds she was submerged in ecstasy, her body quivering with eagerness for the reward his firm cock promised with each rapid thrust.

"C'mon, Mila," he murmured. "You're close. I can feel it." His words ramped up the tension supplied by the rhythm of his hips.

She gulped. "Come with me."

"Nah. Not yet." His voice grew husky. "I love watching you."

Panting, she dug her fingers into his flexing glute muscles. "Alrighty, then."

"Having fun?"

"Big fun." She focused on the glow in his eyes and the hint of a smile on his lips as he wound that spring tighter...and tighter yet.

"Then here we go." He switched gears.

The pace became dizzying. She couldn't breathe, couldn't think, could barely see him as an avalanche of sensation swept away everything but the fireworks erupting deep in her core. She yelled so loud it hurt her ears.

Instead of slowing down, he kept going, prolonging the wave upon wave of tremors rocking her body. And she kept yelling, until he gradually eased up and she slowly sank back onto the mattress and closed her eyes. She hadn't been aware of arching her back.

His ragged breathing evened out and his lips brushed over hers. "Well done."

"Mm." She loosened her grip on his buns and let her arms fall.

"Ready to do it again?"

She rocked her head from side-to-side.

He chuckled. "We'll just have lazy sex, then."

"Mm." She'd figured she was done, but her body seemed to have other ideas. His gentle motion created more interest than she'd thought possible. Slowly she opened her eyes and gazed up at him. "How'd you do it?"

"What?"

She took a quick breath. "Go all in..." She gulped more air. "And not come?"

"I built up to it. The first few times I couldn't hold back. Now I can."

She blinked. "You almost called it quits today."

"I know."

"I would've missed this!"

"You don't miss what you've never had."

"That's a sneaky way to make your point."

"I didn't mean to. You handed me the opening. Besides, it's true."

"Well, now I know what I almost missed, and good luck getting rid of me, cowboy." Yeah, she was getting worked up again. Amazing.

"That's the problem. I don't want to get rid of you."

"Then don't." She wasn't the only one getting excited. His breathing had changed. "We'll start with putting Santa hats on the Beaver Bunch and work our way from there."

"You don't give up easy."

"Are you just finding that out?"

"Oh, I knew it. Considered it a plus."

"Because it is." She stroked his sweaty back. "You're working up a lather."

"For a good cause. You're gonna come again." He picked up the pace.

"Maybe." She rubbed her palm across a thin ridge on his back. A scar from childhood?

"Let's make sure of it." Balancing on one arm, he slid his other hand under her tush and shifted the angle.

"Ohhhh." The soft exclamation came unbidden from her lips as he created a delicious friction that captured her complete attention.

"Like that?"

"Just a little bit."

"Then let's go with it." He got down to business, stoking her furnace with the skill of a master.

If she'd thought she knew all about his bedroom skills after the first few go-rounds, she'd been sadly mistaken. Clearly she'd only scratched the surface.

And she was definitely on the way to another spectacular orgasm. But this time, so was he. She heard it in his soft hum as he moved faster and the catch in his voice as he urged her on.

He wasn't a bystander this time. He was in the fray, with fire in his eyes and sweat beading his forehead. When she let go, shouting at him to join her, he did, calling her name as he drove in and held his ground, his body shaking with the force of his release.

She cradled him in her arms and rejoiced in the beauty of what they could create together. He was willing to be open and vulnerable when they made love.

Surely he could learn to dismantle the other walls he'd built. It would just take time. Her challenge would be learning patience.

<u>27</u>

Cole fetched the groceries and put them away while Mila started on the Santa hats. Leaving fresh produce in the truck would have been a disaster in the summer, but in December with the temperature dropping and a storm coming in, those veggies were fine.

She kept working while he fixed them a couple of turkey sandwiches. She'd made good progress by the time she put the hats aside to have some lunch.

"It won't take much longer." She slid onto a stool. "Thanks for making these. Do I smell apple cider?"

"I warmed it up. Figured that would go better with it looking so wintry outside."

"Great idea."

He set down two steaming mugs. "I didn't bring up the toys. Should I?"

"It makes more sense to take them over to Adam's. He and Tracy are the ones who'll wrap them. He's going to want to reimburse you."

"He can try but he won't succeed." He took the stool next to her and picked up his phone. "I'd better see if they're home and do it after we eat.

Judging from the clouds, the snow could start anytime." He sent a quick text before turning back to his sandwich.

She gestured toward the windows. "I've never been up here when it's snowing. Do you pull down the blinds or leave them up?"

"I usually leave them up so I can watch it fall, unless it's a blizzard. But I'm here alone, so there's nothing to see but me walking around."

"If it's snowing, nobody will be outside peering up at your windows so it doesn't matter what's going on." She bit into her sandwich.

"Oh, I dunno about that. Adam's cabin's on a rise and so's Rio's Swiss chalet. If they wanted to, they could see right into this loft."

"But they'd need binoculars."

"Or a telescope. Like the one Rio has."

"That's right, he does have one. I don't think he'd use it to spy on us but I wouldn't swear to it. So we'll just make sure we keep our clothes on."

"Or pull down the blinds. If I have a choice between watching snow or your beautiful body, it's no contest."

"You won't have to choose. As I've already mentioned, I'm not the type to prance around the house naked even with the blinds down. As I recall, neither are you."

"Not normally, but now that I have you up here, I'm ready to try different venues. The couch would be fun. Closer to the fireplace."

She laughed. "You have a one-track mind."

"And you don't?"

"I'm focused on the Santa hats."

He nudged her knee with his. "Not that focused. When I mentioned the couch your eyes sparkled." His phone pinged and he picked it up. "They're home. He said it's good timing, so I'll take the toys over after we finish eating."

"Have you ever been in their cabin?"

"No, I guess not."

"It's cozy. My dad built it to coax my great-grandma Lucy to move out of the Victorian in town and come live on the ranch with us. It's modeled on the one she grew up in."

"I really wish I'd known your dad." Hell, he wished he'd met them all years ago, especially Mila.

"Luis and I talked about that last night. We both regret that you and Jordan missed out. And now there's Liberty, who won't ever know her grandpa."

"I'll bet he's sad about that."

"He is, but then he said—" She stopped abruptly and dropped her gaze. "I'm an idiot."

"He said he was an idiot?"

"No. Never mind." She looked up. "You should get going. The storm could hit early and you'd be stuck there."

"Not a chance. What did Luis say?"

"Something you don't need to hear."

"Mila."

She looked miserable. "Please don't take this to heart."

"I can't promise that. Just tell me."

"He said that he didn't feel so bad about Liberty not getting to meet her grandpa now that you and I are together."

"I don't follow."

"If Dad had lived, we wouldn't have needed to hire you. You wouldn't be living here, which means this—" She gestured around the loft. "Wouldn't have happened. Chances are *we* wouldn't have happened."

He was stunned.

"See why I didn't want to tell you?"

"Did you mention we're not exactly a done deal?" This was why he never should have kissed her. He'd fudging known it could screw up everybody and everything.

"No. I should have, but I—"

"It's okay. I wouldn't have, either."

"Listen, if it doesn't work out for us, you'll still be here. We'll still be friends. It won't be the end of the world."

He gazed at her. She could say that all day long and maybe she believed it. He didn't. What they'd shared was too intense. Casual friendship wasn't in the cards.

But it could snow any minute and he had toys to deliver. He sucked in a breath. "Do you have Christmas music on your phone?"

"Doesn't everybody?" Then she winced. "Sorry. Yes, I do."

"Then please play it while you're working on the Santa hats. I didn't think of it before, but if you turn on Mannheim Steamroller when you make fudge with Claudie, it stands to reason you'd like to do it while you're sewing those hats."

"I will, at least while you're gone."

"And even when I get back."

"We'll see."

"I'm serious." Leaning over, he gave her a quick kiss. Then he picked up their empty plates and carried them to the kitchen counter.

"Leave those. I just saw a few flakes."

"Okay. I'm outta here." Grabbing his coat and hat, he put them on as he headed out the door.

By the time he was halfway down the steps, a jazzed up version of *Joy to the World* made it through his soundproofing. She must've turned that sucker up to rock concert volume.

The peppy rendition was unlike anything he'd heard before, which meant his visceral reaction was mild. Pausing on the steps, he let himself listen to the energetic sound that Mila loved so much.

He pictured her working on the hat project while she absorbed the dramatic music. Its vibrancy suited her. Could he blend his passion for her into that spirited sound? It was an idea.

The music faded as he reached the bottom of the steps. Fetching the plastic sack of toys, he slung them over his shoulder and set off, lengthening his stride. He could smell the snow.

Flakes drifted down, melting as they landed on his cheeks. He walked faster across the hard-packed yard, passing the mini-hacienda and the steep hill leading up to Rio's A-frame.

Adam and Tracy's log cabin sat on a rise, too. The path was a few yards beyond the one leading to Rio's place. Multicolored lights of a Christmas tree shone through the front window and cedar smoke drifted from the chimney.

The clouds darkened the sky enough for everyone's Christmas lights to come on,

transforming the landscape. A memory surfaced —
walking home from a friend's house in December.
He must've been around nine.

All the neighbors had lights up and a
decorated tree in the front window. Every house
but his. He'd considered going back to his buddy's
place and asking if they'd adopt him. But he
couldn't do that to Jordie, so he'd kept going.

He glanced over at the loft. No lights and
no tree in the window, but Mila was in there
making Santa hats and listening to cranked up
Christmas music. Progress?

When he used the horseshoe knocker on
the cabin's sturdy wooden door, Tracy opened it,
her red hair piled in a haphazard style on top of her
head. Cute.

She grinned "Well, hel-*lo*, Santa!"

That threw him until he remembered the
sack of toys over his shoulder. He managed a smile.
"Have you been a good little girl?"

"Heck, no. Where's the fun in that? Come
on in. I have hot chocolate on the stove."

"Of course you do." Also a cheerful fire,
carols playing, and the living room littered with
rolls of wrapping paper and ribbons. He was in
Christmas hell.

"Hey, buddy!" Adam, wearing a sweatshirt
with Rudolph on the front, came toward him, hand
outstretched. "You have no idea how grateful I am
that you picked up the last of the toys. The
snowstorm could've thrown a spanner in the
works."

"I'm glad Mila and I got 'er done." He shook
Adam's hand and gave him the bag.

"You'd better have a receipt in your pocket."

"Afraid not. Consider it a donation to the cause."

Adam held his gaze. "It'll be easy for me to estimate what you spent. It's not chicken feed."

"I wanted to do it. I know what it's like to be a kid whose parents are…" He cleared his throat. "Struggling."

"Alrighty, then." Emotion flickered in his eyes. "I'm much obliged."

Cole recognized that look. He used to get it all the time as a kid. "Listen, I'd better—"

"Whipped cream or marshmallows?" Tracy called from the kitchen.

"You know what? I appreciate the offer but I should probably shove off. The snow—"

"It'll do the lazy flake thing for a while," Adam said. "If you won't take a check, at least drink some hot chocolate. You won't regret it."

He could refuse and ruin the moment or accept and employ his survival skills. He raised his voice. "Whipped cream, please. Thanks, Tracy."

As he took off his hat and coat, he breathed in the scent of that hot chocolate. By focusing on the sweet drink and the two kind people in the cabin, he'd make it through.

<u>28</u>

Mila was so absorbed in her project and her Mannheim playlist pouring from her phone that she didn't hear Cole come in until the couch cushion moved and there he was, sitting next to her minus his hat and coat.

She jumped and grabbed her phone. "Sorry. I'll—"

"Don't." Moving closer, he closed his hand over hers. "Leave it on."

"Okay, but I can turn it down."

He shook his head as he picked up the Santa hat in her lap and set it aside. Then he stood and drew her to her feet. "Will you make love with me?"

"With the music on?"

"Yes."

Her heart stuttered. He was trying. "But it's so loud. Wouldn't you rather—"

"I want it loud, the way you like it."

That almost started the waterworks, but she managed to hold them back. Gulping, she nodded. Phone in hand, filling the space with the sounds of Christmas, she walked into the bedroom with him.

She laid it on the bedside table as he closed the doors and came toward her. She started to pull off her sweater.

"Let me." He undressed her slowly and reverently before scooping her up and laying her on the bed they'd purposely left unmade. His gaze locked with hers, he took off his clothes and rolled on the condom with the same measured pace.

He didn't speak as he climbed into bed and moved over her. But his ragged breathing and the emotion in his gray eyes spoke volumes as he thrust deep. He was making a new memory. With her.

Wrapping him in her arms, she twined her legs around his, eager for every part of her to touch every part of him. He loved her with long, sure strokes, creating their magic connection again and again, building toward a climax.

They would share this one. Her body knew it. Her heart did, too. Was this the beginning of a change? Did she dare hope?

He pumped faster, increasing the tension as their moist bodies slid ever closer to release. He knew her well now. Shifting slightly, he touched off the first wave and she gasped.

"*Yes.*" His voice was gruff as he picked up the pace and hurtled them both toward glory. "*Yes!*"

She let go with a cry and he followed right after, driving deep and shuddering as their world exploded, shattering their boundaries and creating, for a few precious seconds, one body, one heart, one soul.

She lay beneath him panting.

"The music." He gulped in air. "It just stopped."

"That's...the end...of my...playlist."

"Oh. Not very long."

She couldn't help smiling. "Long enough."

"Guess so."

"Did you get what you came for?"

He sucked in another breath. "You probably think I'm nuts."

"I think you're working on this issue. That makes me very happy." She slid her hands up his sweaty back. In the process she brushed over the thin line of the scar she'd felt before. Then she found another one.

"I tried to keep at least some of my attention on the music. That's why I wanted it loud." His mouth tilted in a half-smile. "Tougher than I thought. You're potent."

"Think you made a new Christmas memory?"

"For sure I made a hot new memory. That happens every time we hop into this bed. Whether it's truly a Christmas memory, I can't say. Maybe." Leaning down, he kissed her. "Thanks for indulging me." He eased away and left the bed.

"Anytime, cowboy." She got out of bed, too. "I'm thinking I'll take a shower and put on my jammies."

He laughed. "You brought some?"

"I did, but now I'm wondering if they'll cause you a problem."

"Only if they're hard to get off."

"They're easy to get off, but they're kind of Christmasy." She dug them out of her duffle and carried them toward the bathroom.

"Let's see 'em."

She held up the long-sleeved top so he could examine the theme of evergreens, wreaths and red trucks with a pine tree in the back.

"That's not too bad. I just spent almost an hour looking at Adam's sweatshirt, so this is way easier."

"The Rudolph one?"

"That's it."

"How about Tracy? She has holiday sweaters and sweatshirts, too."

"Hers was Frosty. I can handle him. When you get right down to it, he has nothing to do with Christmas."

"True. So you're okay with these? I don't have to wear them. I can borrow your sweats again."

He studied the images. "I think you should wear them. They look like they're more comfortable than my sweats and it's good for me to practice desensitizing myself to red and green."

"It sounds like you're trying to give yourself color blindness."

"Believe it or not, I used to envy people who are color blind. Then I realized that comes with a whole new set of problems."

"Do traffic lights bother you?"

"No, ma'am. I've worked through that."

"On your own?"

"If you mean did I have counseling, I tried it once. Didn't care for it."

She wasn't surprised. Counseling wouldn't do much good if he refused to talk about what he'd been through.

He was the exact opposite of her ex, who'd played on her sympathies by detailing all the mistreatment he'd endured. Cole, who'd likely experienced far worse, kept it locked down.

She laid her jammies on the counter. "Then I guess I'll wear these. If they start bugging you, let me know."

"I won't let that happen."

Yep, he was Iron Man. She picked up a scrunchie to hold back her hair. "Mind if I take a shower?"

"Go right ahead. I'd join you, but I'm not starving this time. So we might end up in bed again and I don't want to wear out my welcome."

She laughed. "You think five times in ten hours might be pushing it?"

"I'm just sayin'. I've heard tales of newlywed sex that left them in sad shape."

"Then how about this? Let's see if we can shower together without ending up in bed."

"Could be a challenge."

"Are you up to it?"

"What the fudge. Sure. I'll turn on the water." He stepped over to the spacious shower. Instead of a curtain, a glass block partition and a sunken tiled floor kept the water in. He twisted the handle and held his hand under the spray.

"I mean, you did build a suspiciously large shower. I didn't mention that the first time, but—"

"I confess I've pictured you in it with me." He moved back and gestured toward the opening. "After you. Adjust it if the temp's not right."

She grabbed a washcloth and stepped under the warm spray. Determined to tend to business, she picked up the bar of soap from its holder and lathered up her washcloth. "Come on in. The water's fine."

"Glad you approve."

The minute he ducked inside, she reached out, unable to stop herself from running her hand over his broad chest.

Laughing, he caught her wrist. "This is how we'll end up in bed. You should probably keep your hands to yourself."

"You, too. And your mouth."

He pulled her close and took the sudsy washcloth. "I can't. You're too delicious." He nuzzled the side of her damp neck as he ran the washcloth over her back. "I intend to do a better job washing this time though. This morning I wouldn't say we were exactly washed."

"Good enough."

"But not thorough. I intend to be thorough this go round. Also, I just realized something."

She wrapped her arms around his slick body as the warm water sluicing over her, arousing every inch of her skin. "There's no such thing as a quick shower when we're in here together?"

"That, too, but as long as we don't go back to bed and make love afterward, there's nothing wrong with me giving you a little treat while we're in here. I'll barely have to touch you."

She quivered at the mere suggestion. "That's embarrassingly true. But then you get worked up and—"

"Never mind me." Turning her around so her back was to him, he massaged her breasts with the soapy washcloth before stroking it over each of her arms. "I'm saving myself. Tonight we're going to do it on the couch by the fire."

"No fair talking sexy in the shower."

"You're right. Let's get down to business. Spread your legs, please."

She did, and he washed between them, front and back, nearly making her come with that warm washcloth. Crouching down, he ran it over her legs and instructed her to grab his shoulder while he scrubbed each foot.

Tossing the washcloth on a nearby rack, he grasped her upper arms and turned her slowly under the spray until all the soap was gone.

"Thank you. Excellent job." And she was on fire, as if he didn't know it.

"Not done." Dropping to his knees in front of her, he cupped her tush and began licking the drops away from a very sensitive spot.

She didn't last long under that assault. When she started to come, she grabbed his shoulders.

"I've got you." His grip tightened, holding her fast as he sucked gently, driving her right out of her mind. Her moans ricocheted against the tiled walls, making it sound like an orgy in progress.

In a way it was. She'd never been loved this much in one day, never felt like her body was a temple where her lover worshipped her.

Her words came back to her. *If it doesn't work out for us, you'll still be here. We'll still be friends. It won't be the end of the world.*

Who was she kidding? Maybe he'd hold it together, but her world would shatter into a million pieces.

29

Cole should have insisted on washing himself, because guaranteed she'd turn him on no matter how much she tried not to. But she wanted to do it and he couldn't argue with her premise — she was as fascinated with his body as he was with hers. She'd promised not to touch his cock.

And…okay, it was nice to have her wash him. He felt physically cared for in a way he'd never experienced. "You're good at this."

"Adam and I helped clean up the little ones."

"You have a lot more territory to cover with me."

"And I'm a happy explorer." She began crooning *This Land Is Your Land* as she washed his chest and abs.

"Funny lady."

"We used to sing to the kids to make them settle down."

"It's having the opposite effect on me."

She glanced down. "So I see. I'll move around back. I didn't try that the first time. Maybe that will help."

"It should. You can't get into much mischief in that position."

"Oh, you might be surprised." She circled him and went to work on his shoulders. Then her washcloth slowed. "Hey, what did you do to your back?"

He went still. Dear God. He'd turned his back on her a few times, admittedly from more of a distance, but she hadn't said anything. He must've decided they weren't noticeable anymore.

Or he just desperately wanted to believe it. What did he know? It wasn't like he spent time looking at his back in the mirror.

"Cole?"

"It's an old injury."

"I can tell. What happened?"

He'd concocted a lie that he'd used in the rare times someone had asked. He didn't tend to go shirtless, especially in the apartment he'd shared with Jordie. When he'd been in a relationship with a woman, he'd avoided instances where she could see his back.

Until now, in this big ol' shower he'd created for two. Until along came a woman who wasn't satisfied with skimming the surface. Wasn't that exactly what he'd hoped for? *Now what, genius? Gonna lie to her?*

No. But maybe he could diffuse the situation.

Letting out a sigh, he turned around. "It's not important what happened. It was a long time ago. What's in the past is best left in the past."

Her gaze was steady. "It wasn't an accident, was it?"

"No."

"Someone hit you with something. Hard enough to draw blood."

His heart thumped painfully. He managed a careless shrug. "Shit happens."

"How old were you?"

He took her by the shoulders as warm water cascaded around them, filling the enclosure with steam. Droplets caught on her eyelashes. "Mila." The words came out rougher than he meant them to. "Let it go. Please."

For a long moment she just looked at him. Then she took a shaky breath. "I guess I could do that."

He was dizzy with relief. "Thank you."

"And then what?"

They weren't out of the woods, after all. "We continue to do what we do best, love each other."

"Am I supposed to pretend those scars don't exist?"

"You'll forget about them. I have." Mostly true.

"Really?"

"Sure. When you started washing my back, I didn't think about it until you said something."

"What about the time it happened? Have you forgotten that, too?"

His stomach pitched. "I don't think about it."

"You block it out."

It was not a question. More of an indictment. "Yes."

"Just like you blocked out the music and the decorations in the market today?"

"Something like that." He could see she was headed back to her argument about missing out. He'd rather not go there again. "Tell you what. Let's table this for now, dry off and go check on the snow."

Her troubled frown broke his heart. He wanted to bring her only smiles and joy. Maybe he should have told that lie, after all.

She studied him for a moment longer. "Okay." She handed him the washcloth. "I need to put the sweet potatoes in the oven and prep the chicken. Meet you in the kitchen." Stepping out on the bathmat, she lifted a towel from the rack, wrapped herself in it and left the bathroom.

He didn't kid himself that was the end of the discussion. She had more to say and he doubted he was going to like it. Fudge it all, would those old scars turn out to be his undoing?

He really had temporarily forgotten about them. When he was focused on Mila, everything else faded, especially the bad old days.

He'd been in the shower long enough that his fingertips had started to wrinkle. He gave himself a few more swipes with the washcloth so she'd have a chance to put on her jammies and leave the bedroom. The next time they talked, he planned to be wearing a shirt.

Not that covering his back would help. Evidently this moment would have come sooner or later, so maybe it was good to deal with it now. The next challenge was getting past it.

He'd created the lie about his scars when he was on his first construction job years ago and they were more obvious. A bucket of paint had fallen from a trestle and doused him. He'd taken off his shirt, washed it with a hose and put it back on wet.

In the process, one of the guys had asked him about his back. He'd claimed he'd been crawling under a barbed wire fence to escape an angry bull. Mila didn't deserve to hear that half-assed lie.

She wanted to make things work between them as much as he did. Maybe he could convince her to back off the subject. He'd made love to her while her favorite Christmas music played. That should count for something, right?

Her Christmas-themed jammies would be another test he would pass with fudging flying colors. Ha, ha. The images on them didn't bother him. He'd just ignore the red and green color scheme. It would be good practice.

Switching off the water, he left the shower and took the other bath towel. He'd had two on the rack from the day he'd installed it. Also two washcloths, plus two hand towels on hooks by the sink.

Although it had taken him months to admit it to himself, he'd always intended to share this loft. The only candidate had been the woman currently in residence. It was a wonder he hadn't equipped the bathroom with twin sinks.

He could hear her moving around in the kitchen, opening the fridge, running water as she rinsed off the potatoes and the chicken. Music to his ears.

He fetched clean sweats from his dresser, put them on and tucked a condom in his pocket. He might have just ruined any chance to make love in front of the fire tonight, but he'd hope for the best.

Next he reached for a sweatshirt. Out of sight, out of mind, at least until he took it off again. He shoved his arms in the sleeves and was about to pop his head through the neck opening when he changed his mind.

He hadn't looked at his back in months, maybe even years. How bad was it? He should check. Mila had brought a hand mirror with her, likely to see all sides of her hair. Jordie had always had a mirror like that for the same reason.

Returning to the bathroom, he picked up the mirror, turned his back to the cabinet above the sink and winced. Yeah, those damn scars were still visible — four thin white lines. Three ran from side to side. The fourth angled from his shoulder to his waist.

He shuddered, put down the mirror and turned around as a familiar queasiness churned in his gut. Bracing both hands on the counter, he bowed his head and forced himself to take several deep breaths.

As he dragged moist air into his lungs, he called up an image of loping Sparky through a meadow of pink fireweed. His first ride on his first-ever horse. The beauty of that moment gradually beat down the nightmare, sending it to the dungeon where it belonged.

Sparky had been a godsend, offering him a chance to work off steam at a dead run, meander down a shade-dappled path, or quietly bask in the majesty of a sunrise. Riding his horse helped keep his demons at bay.

Questions about his scars did not. If he'd wondered whether he could handle telling her, he had the answer.

A few more deep breaths and he was ready to put on his sweatshirt. A sweet aroma drifted through the barn doors. Did baking sweet potatoes smell like that? If so, he really had been missing out.

Running his fingers through his damp hair, he walked into the main room in his bare feet. He wasn't deliberately trying to sneak around. He just needed to get his bearings before announcing his presence.

Mila had returned to the couch to work on a Santa hat. Her phone rested near her hip, softly playing Mannheim Steamroller as she stitched the white furry strip back on. Looked like the last one.

Blocking out the red and green decorating her jammies, he concentrated on the snow falling steadily past the windows, the aroma of baking sweet potatoes, and lantern light gleaming on Mila's dark hair as she concentrated on those tiny stitches. Even the faint music was a positive, now that he associated it with loving her.

He wanted this, wanted it more than he'd ever wanted anything. But could he have it? The jury was still out.

She glanced up, the look in her eyes difficult to read. "Almost done."

"So I see." A pain shot through his chest. When she finished, she'd have no obligation to stay. Was she planning her escape?

Her expression softened. "I'm not leaving tonight."

"That's good." No point denying she'd guessed his thoughts. He walked over and settled next to her. "I don't want you to."

"I don't want to, either, but I probably should go back tomorrow."

"Oh?" The pain in his chest returned. She'd just chopped one night out of the plan. "Why is that?"

"I can't speak for you, but I need time to think. To process. Normally I'd talk this out with Claudie, but obviously I can't do that. Instead I'll take a long ride on Sol."

He glanced out the window at the curtain of falling snow. He should have known she'd use riding to work things out in her head. So did he. "Tomorrow might not be a good day for that."

"Or it could be perfect. I checked the weather and the snow should stop around midnight. I love riding over fresh snow."

Sounded nice, but she clearly wasn't inviting him along. Maybe she'd accepted his refusal to tell his sob story, though, since she hadn't brought up the subject first thing out of the box.

That didn't mean they were hunky-dory, though. Just the opposite. Evidently she felt the need to distance herself. If he had to guess, he'd say she wanted to get clear on whether to continue this relationship. In the process, she'd give him time to reconsider his stance.

He sucked in air. "Is this what people call a soft breakup?"

"Absolutely not." She stuck the needle in the furry part, put the hat aside and turned to him. "I want to be with you."

"Except you're leaving early."

"Because I need to assess where we are. Where I am."

"Looks to me like we're both sitting on the couch in my loft." A voice in his head corrected it to *our loft.*

She made a face. "You know what I mean."

"I do. Just trying to lighten the moment."

"A lot's happened in a short time."

"Yes, ma'am."

"It started as a strong attraction and, let's be honest, it quickly ramped up to good old-fashioned lust."

"You'll get no argument on that."

"But now it's...." Her voice trailed off.

The warm, steady light in her eyes pushed the air right out of his lungs. She sat there just looking at him, her breathing shallow and her cheeks pink.

Alrighty, then. He'd be a fudging fool if he let this moment pass, if he didn't say what she almost had. "It's love."

30

Damn it, she was gonna cry.

"I love you, Mila." Cole turned sideways and took her hands in his. "While you're out on your ride, please add that into the mix. I love you."

She blinked quickly and staved off the worst of it. A few tears still dribbled down.

He leaned over and kissed her damp cheeks. "I didn't mean to make you cry."

"It's happy tears." She sniffed. "I love you, too. I just figured saying it was counterproductive."

That startled a laugh out of him. "Not the word I would have chosen."

She squeezed his hands and scooted closer. "Love muddies the waters."

"You see mud, I see a miracle. You love me." His eyes blazed with emotion. "You fudging *love me.* Can you imagine how that makes me feel?"

"I can. Oh, I can." She locked onto the passion in his gaze, her heart beating fast. "And I really want—"

"Babies?"

"Yes, eventually, but what I—"

"I told you I'd be bad at this father thing, but I was forgetting something."

"What I said about you taking care of Jordan?"

"Not that. I forgot that next summer, Liberty arrives on the scene."

She got it, now. "You can practice being a dad."

"Damn straight. Jordie and Luis will show me how it's done."

"Great idea." Not what she wanted to talk about, but still a positive.

"Isn't it? I've watched my sister work with clients who don't know a hackamore from their hind quarters. They're harder to train than the horse. If she can handle them, she can train me."

He'd sidetracked her and turned her insides to mush with this new subject. "It won't take long. I was never worried about the baby issue."

"Well, I was. But Jordie won't let me fail. She knows babies scare the hell out of me. She's the only one I've ever held, and I was terrified I'd do something wrong."

Clearly he wasn't kidding. The fear in his voice was real, and it gave her another clue to his past. At four, his terror probably had been justified. If he had done something wrong, he likely would've been severely punished.

But he didn't want her to know about that, or why he had scars on his back, or how they were related to his Christmas phobia. He'd given her some information but not the critical piece.

His gaze searched hers. Then his chest heaved. "I interrupted you a while ago. Twice."

"You did." Whoa. This was new.

"I have a hunch you were trying to bring up a different subject."

Amazing. Unexpected. "Is that why you interrupted me?"

"Yep." He brought her hands to his lips and kissed her fingers. "I've decided to man up to it." Lifting his head, he looked into her eyes, a crease of worry between his brows. "Forgive me?"

Her heart swelled. "Always."

"It's a bad habit." He tucked her hands behind his neck, slid his arms around her waist and drew her closer. "I don't want to do that with you. I want you to call me on it."

"All right." She took a breath. Might as well seize the moment. "Are you afraid if you tell me I'll tell the others? Because I won't "

"I know." He hesitated, glanced away. When he faced her again, the haunted look was back in his eyes. "Have you ever watched a movie and then wished you hadn't?"

"I think we've all done that."

"You don't want to see this movie. Nobody should."

She stared at him, confused by *nobody should.* "But Jordan knows."

His grip on her hands tightened imperceptibly. "She doesn't."

"How's that possible?"

"I'm not the type to go around shirtless."

So he'd protected his little sister from the movie he didn't want her to see. He'd protected everyone, now that she thought about it. Her brothers loved pulling off their shirts and pouring water over their heads when it was hot. She'd never seen Cole do that.

"Then why did you let me wash your back?"

"I shouldn't have. I had this stupid idea that since you'd glimpsed it a few times and hadn't asked, you couldn't see them. I haven't checked in ages."

"I also felt them. At least a couple."

"Did you decide to wash my back so you could investigate?"

"Not at first, but once I was there, yeah, I wanted to find out what was going on."

He groaned. "I almost wish I'd...."

"Lied to me?"

"Yes!" He sucked in a breath. "No. I can't lie to you."

"What would you have said?"

"The same thing I've told anyone who happens to see my back for some reason. I crawled under a barbed wire fence to escape an angry bull."

"Did you tell that to Jordan?"

"No. I don't lie to my sister. Besides, it wouldn't have worked. She'd have pestered me for details."

"Good grief. You've been on guard for *years*." And he'd let down his guard in the shower. She'd hang onto that tiny bit of success.

"Worth it." He sighed. "My coping mechanisms might seem weird but they get me through."

She could argue that point but listening was more important right now. "So you keep your shirt on and block out Christmas." Which told her he'd been hit during the holidays.

"That's about the size of it. I've ignored Christmas for so long it didn't register as something I'd need to deal with when I moved here. I'll keep working on it. Like right now, I'm not bothered by your jammies."

"You're okay with the red and green?"

"I am because I'm not focused on it. I'm focused on you. That's how I build tolerance."

"Tolerance?" Her mind rebelled and the word popped out. "Sorry. I just...."

"That's not what you want to hear."

"It's not about me or what I want to hear."

"It is about you. I'm playing for all the marbles. That means I need to get this Christmas thing under control."

She wanted to shake him until his teeth rattled. And then rock him in her arms until he quit torturing himself and confided in someone, preferably her. Would he ever do that? "It sounds exhausting."

"I'm used to it."

Oh, she bet he was. "Just so you know, I'm not a fragile flower. None of us are after losing our dad." Both her dads, actually. "That wasn't a great movie, either."

"I'm sure it wasn't. Luis said he went quickly, but that's its own kind of hell."

"It was. Like I said, crappy movie, but at least we watched it together. That was huge."

He gave her a crooked smile. "Trying to tell me something?"

"Subtle, huh?"

"No."

"Bottom line, I'll watch your movie with you. Anytime. Anywhere."

"Appreciate the offer, but the theater's closed." He said it gently, but his jaw tightened.

Considering how many years he'd been committed to this path, she wasn't surprised by his response. Disappointed, but not surprised.

He took a breath. "On the other hand, we can still have dinner and a show compliments of the Beaver Bunch."

Her disappointment melted. "I'll take that deal."

"Thank you." Leaning over he gave her a tender kiss. And lingered.

She savored the moment. Had they made progress? A tiny bit, and a man who could bestow such loving kisses wouldn't stay closed off forever.

_31_

Turned out Cole liked sweet potatoes topped with sour cream. The chicken and veggie stir-fry he'd helped Mila fix was delicious and the chocolate cupcakes they'd bought at the market's bakery tasted amazing.

Rufus, Buster and Shorty, looking cute as hell in their Santa hats, had provided lively entertainment the whole time they ate. While Mila had finished the last hat, Cole had put together a playlist for the little guys, one that he'd designed to last through dinner.

At the end, he'd included the jug band's rendition of Jason Aldean's *You Make It Easy*. He wasn't above tugging on her heartstrings with a tender love song.

Every time he thought about her leaving in the morning, his insides hollowed out. When she was here, anything was possible, but when she was gone....

They'd almost polished off the cupcakes when the tune started. She put hers down and glanced at him. "How did you know?"

"Know what?"

"That I love this one."

"Lucky guess." *Really* lucky. He'd take it as a sign. The jug band hadn't recorded many love songs. Tunes like *The Devil Went Down to Georgia* were more their speed. He'd had to talk them into *You Make It Easy.*

She reached for his hand. "How come you didn't play this before?"

He wove his fingers through hers, enjoying the image of their clasped hands. Then he looked up. "Didn't want to be pushy."

"But now you want to be?"

"Lady, I intend to be the pushiest cowboy you've ever come across." That made her laugh. "I mean it."

"Alrighty, then. Is this song the beginning of that effort?"

"Guess you could say that." He couldn't stop looking at her. Her expressive eyes almost made it possible to read her mind, and the message he was getting filled him with hope. "I'm nuts about you, Mila."

She leaned closer and lowered her voice to a sultry murmur. "*Yo tambien estoy loco por ti, mi amor.*"

"I have no idea what you said except for three words but it sounded promising."

"I said *those beavers love their Santa hats.*"

"No, you didn't." Laughing, he slid off his stool. Whatever she'd said indicated the meal was over and the loving would begin. "I heard *loco.* I know that one."

"I said *let's leave the dishes.*"

"Nope, not that either." He scooped her into his arms and carried her over to the couch. "But it fits the tone of whatever you said."

She wound her arms around his neck. "I suppose you think you can haul me anywhere you want."

"Sure do, especially when you lean in and murmur indecent suggestions." He deposited her on the couch and followed her down, nestling between her thighs.

"There was nothing indecent about what I said."

"I don't know that, now do I?" Bracing on one arm, he lifted up, slid his hand under the soft material of her top and cupped her breast.

Her breath caught. "Are you planning to do something indecent?"

"Not on purpose." He brushed his thumb over her tight nipple and watched her eyes darken. "I'm not sure what that means anymore, but I plan to do a decent job of driving you crazy."

"You think that's what I said?"

"Maybe." He nudged her gently with his hips. "Am I right?"

"Almost." She wrapped her legs around his. "I said that I'm crazy about you, too." She tightened her hold.

And he wasn't in charge anymore. So not in charge. "Careful."

Her eyes sparkled as she loosened her grip. "Just evening the score."

"Fair enough." He took a long, slow breath. "How do I say *I'm crazy about you*?"

"*Estoy loco por ti.*"

"*Estoy loco por ti.*"

"That's good."

"And I am. *Muy loco.* How about *let's get naked*?"

"Yes, let's." She reached for the hem of her top.

"I meant, how do you say it?"

She paused with her top pulled halfway up. "You want a Spanish lesson *now*?"

"I want to love you in Spanish and this is a teachable moment."

She smiled. "That's...*muy adorable.*"

"So? How do you say it?"

"Short or long version?"

"Short."

"*A desnudarse!*"

"*A desnudarse!*"

"*Muevete para que pueda hacerio.*"

"What's that mean?"

"Move so I can do it."

"Oh." He rolled away and stood so he could shuck his sweats while muttering *a desnudarse* under his breath.

"*Tienes un condon?*"

"*Si, seniorita.*"

"Listen to you, getting comfy with the language!"

"Didn't need a translation for that one." Coward that he was, he made sure he was facing her as he took off his sweatshirt.

Not that he'd eliminated the issue. She'd said that she'd felt the scars when stroking his naked back. An ancient rage, one he'd buried deep, stretched and flexed its claws. Closing his eyes, he dipped his head and took a deep breath.

"*Mi amor.*" Her soft voice tickled his ear as she slid her arms around him from behind and pressed her warm body against his back, his glutes, his thighs. "*Te amo. Te amo mucho.*"

With a groan, he turned in her arms and gathered her close. He didn't have to ask what she'd said or why she'd left the couch and embraced him that way. He knew.

Gazing into the velvet brown of her eyes, he fought against breaking down. "*Te amo, mi amor.*" He forced the words through his tight throat. He sounded like he had a bad cold. "*Te amo mucho.*"

She wiggled against him. "*Amame.*"

He read the meaning in the flush on her cheeks, the intensity in her eyes and the rapid beat of her heart that thumped so hard he could feel it against his chest. No language barrier, there.

But to be sure he understood, she dangled a condom in front of his face. She must've fished it out of his sweats pocket.

He snorted, and suddenly he was laughing so hard she had to help him open the foil package. *This woman.* She made him feel all the things, whether he wanted to or not.

Still laughing, he lowered her to the couch. Or maybe she got there herself and dragged him down. He lost track, but somehow he ended up in her arms and his delighted cock proceeded to have the time of its life.

He paid no attention to the fireplace. He was too busy watching pleasure light her up, too busy controlling his climax so he could give her two of them. *Amame.* What a beautiful word.

So many beautiful words. He would learn them all. Maybe this week.

Then she tightened around his cock for the second time. He let out a cry of pure joy as he jumped into the swirl of bliss with her, holding on as he called out her name over and over and over. Mila, Mila, Mila. Incredible Mila. The woman who loved him, scars and all.

32

Mila had figured leaving Cole in the morning would be a challenge, but she'd underestimated how much she'd want to stay. The loft had never felt cozier and Cole had never looked more appealing. It didn't help that he didn't want her to go, either.

Her duffle sat beside the door, ready for her to stash it in her truck since she didn't want to alert Claudie until later in the day. She was dressed in jeans and a warm sweater for her ride. All she had to do was walk out.

Instead she dawdled at the kitchen island drinking yet another cup of coffee and eating zucchini bread. Breakfast was essentially over, but they'd bought a loaf of it when they'd picked out the cupcakes and it tasted perfect with coffee.

She accepted the freshly cut slice he held her way. "At this rate we'll go through the whole thing."

"It's made from a veggie. It's good for you."

"Not that good. It's loaded with sugar."

"So are you and you're great for me." He leaned over and kissed her cheek.

She gave him a gentle shove. "Don't start or I'll never go."

"So don't go. Nobody's expecting you, are they?"

"No. Not even Claudie. She thinks I'm coming back tomorrow."

"Then do that and take your ride tomorrow, too. The snow will still be nice."

She shook her head. "We need all of tomorrow and the next day to make sure we get the fudge done and packaged up. Today's the right time for a ride."

"What if you get everything sorted out early? Then what?"

"I was thinking I'd pay a visit to the Dazzling Damsels. I usually try to do that every week or so, but now it's been at least three since I dropped in for afternoon tea."

"Then maybe I'll take Adam up on that poker game."

"What poker game?"

"Tracy's spending the day with her folks and Jordie's going over to your mom's to collect some baby stuff she's been saving, so Adam and Luis decided to get up a game. I told him I couldn't make it, but I guess I can."

"You'll have fun."

"And you'll have fun with the Damsels. That actually sounds like a good idea. They like me. They'll tell you to snatch me up before someone else does."

She chuckled. "I'm sure they will. Tia Kat says if she were twenty years younger, she'd go for you herself."

"Only twenty years? Isn't she eighty-four?"

"If you'd seen a picture of her at sixty-four, you wouldn't be saying that. Guys in their forties were begging her to go out with them. Mom told me she had one boyfriend who was thirty-six."

"Incredible."

"She was a babe. Still is."

'You'll always be a babe, too."

"Not like her. She has the Bridger genes. Great-grandma Lucy was a beauty into her nineties. The women in my family tend to be more...full-figured."

"I've noticed." He did a slow, blatantly sexual scan of her body. "I like it."

"No fair." Now she was tingling all over.

"I never said I'd be fair." He met her gaze. "I want one more night."

Damn, he was sexy. She hesitated.

"Leave your stuff here. Take that ride, visit the Damsels, then come back."

"I want to, but...."

"I'll make it worth your while."

"When you look at me like that I can't think straight." Which was the point, wasn't it? She needed alone time to get clarity on this relationship. "Are you okay with me saying maybe?"

"I'll take maybe instead of no any day."

"Then I'll see how things go." She made herself put down her coffee mug and get off the stool.

He stood, too. "I don't think I ever properly thanked you for making the Santa hats. The guys look cute in them."

"I appreciate you saying that."

"I'm not trying to butter you up. I mean it."

She raised her eyebrows.

"Okay, a little bit of buttering going on, but I really do like how they look."

"Good. Me, too."

"Do I get a goodbye kiss?"

"Only if you promise to keep your hands in your pockets."

"Hey, I wouldn't—"

"I'm not saying you would mean to, but—"

"All right. Done." He tucked them in deep.

She did the same.

He glanced at her and shook his head. "This is ridiculous."

"Maybe so, but we have a history of turning a kiss into a horizontal two-step. I'm not taking any chances." She closed the distance between them, stood on tiptoe and kissed him lightly on the mouth.

Then she quickly backed away because she instantly craved more.

His eyes fluttered open. "That's it?"

"That's it." The longing in his eyes tore her up. "See you later." She put on her coat, left it unzipped, crammed on her Stetson and picked up her duffle.

"Wait. Why not just leave it?"

"Better not. I'll stick it in my truck like I planned and grab it if I come back."

He sighed. "Okay. Enjoy your ride. Tell the Damsels I said hi."

"I will. Hope you win at poker. 'Bye." She opened the door and stepped out on the landing.

"Be careful on the stairs." His words followed her out.

"You bet!" She closed the door and started down, forcing herself to go slow when she wanted to take them fast. She had to get away quickly before she gave in to the urge to forget the whole thing, go back inside and hurl herself into his arms.

She'd never been so crazy about a man. But she'd made a mistake last time and she by damn wouldn't do it again. She desperately needed this ride.

Hers were the first footsteps in a pristine layer of snow at the bottom of the stairs. The sunlight hadn't reached that area yet, but the expanse beyond sparkled as if overlaid with diamonds.

As she created a path over to her truck, she glanced at the mini-hacienda draped in glittering white. Fragrant cedar smoke rose from the chimney. Claudie had a fire going.

Sadness gripped her. She longed to confide in her sister, but any discussion would have to include information she couldn't share. She'd have to pour her heart out to Sol, instead.

Tossing her duffle in her truck, she walked back the way she'd come, passing the stairs to the loft without turning her head.

The snow in front of the barn's double doors was well trampled. Adam and whoever had barn duty with him today had been and gone. The pasture was empty, so they must've decided against turning the horses out.

Lucky for her. She wouldn't have to take time to fetch Sol, and she was itching to be off. He whinnied a greeting when he spied her coming.

"Got a job for you, buddy." She grabbed a lead rope and halter from a hook by his stall and stepped inside. "I need to work through a high stakes situation, and you're just the one to help me do it."

The palomino's ears pricked forward.

"You know exactly what I'm talking about, don'tcha?" She slipped on the halter and gave him a nose rub. "It's that guy who lives upstairs." She glanced toward the ceiling and calculated the distance to the front of the barn. They were standing under Cole's kitchen.

The barn had added significance since the renovation. Knowing he was up there, likely washing up after their breakfast, she could feel his presence as if he were standing next to her.

She could text him, invite him to come down and saddle Sparky. They could enjoy this glorious snow-spangled morning together.

She heaved a sigh. "C'mon." She clipped the lead rope on Sol's halter. "We're outta here."

He was generally a cooperative horse, and this morning he was super accommodating, standing perfectly still as she tacked him up. Maybe he understood this was an important journey or maybe he was simply looking forward to fresh air and sunshine.

She tucked snow pads into his shoes to keep him from getting the stuff packed in his hooves. When she swung into the saddle and headed for the gate, a ripple of excitement passed through his body.

"I'm excited too, buddy. This'll be good for both of us."

He gave a snort of agreement, sending out twin clouds of moist air.

As she passed by the barn, she'd be visible to Cole if he happened to be looking. She'd bet he was. She didn't glance up.

Once through the gate, she let out a breath and nudged Sol into a slow trot. While a run across the meadow would feel great, she wouldn't risk it. Instead she took a trail that she knew well, one along the edge of the meadow that was less likely to have buried hazards.

Swathed in snow, the Flint Creek Range stood in stark contrast to a sky so blue it hurt her eyes. Sun-drenched slopes alternated with shaded purple crevices. She drank in the beauty... and wished Cole was there to share it with her.

"Fudge it all, Sol. I miss him!"

Sol knickered in response.

"But here's the thing. He keeps saying it's better if I don't know what he's been through. I *really* disagree with that. I also don't like his coping strategy. Numbing himself to all kinds of experiences isn't healthy. What do you think?"

Sol glanced back at her, which made her laugh. "Yeah, like I have to ask. It's *no bueno.*"

And she had a problem. Cole had shown no signs of changing his mind on either point. What if he never did? What if that was how he lived for the rest of his life? Could she deal with it?

"I love him, Sol. And I want him to change his tune. But everyone knows you don't get involved with someone thinking they'll change, or worse, that you can change them."

Sol let out a big sigh.

"Exactly. If I want to be with him, I have to accept him as he is."

They rode along in silence except for the crisp sound of Sol's hooves breaking through the snow. Even the meadow on her left and the forest on her right were quiet, except for the occasional plop when a hunk of snow fell from a branch.

"On top of it, this is Christmas, when my family is doing so much better than last Christmas. We have Luis and Jordan's baby news. Adam and Tracy are blissfully happy. *I* want to be happy."

And she was, whenever she was in Cole's arms. When they made love, she could block out the issues. A chill ran down her spine. Was that how *she* wanted to live?

_33_

Cole's head wasn't in the game. Ironically, he couldn't seem to lose.

"*Chingao!*" Luis had been the last one to stay in. He stared in disbelief as Cole apologetically laid down a royal flush to beat his full house.

Rio whistled in surprise. "I've never seen luck like you've had today, buddy."

He gathered up the chips and added them to the stacks in front of him. "Me, neither. I've had winning streaks, but nothing like this." He grimaced. "Sorry."

"Hey, don't feel bad. It's just your day." Adam grinned as he shuffled the deck. "Maybe my sis is your good luck charm."

"Could be." He'd certainly been thinking about her constantly, which should have affected his performance at the poker table. Maybe it had, in a good way.

"I could use another beer." Monty pushed back his chair. "Can I get anybody else one?"

"Me." Zay got up. "In fact, I vote we take a break and bring out some chips. Losing makes me hungry."

Rio stood and glanced at Adam. "Got any of Mom and Greta's Christmas cookies? I could go for some of those, too."

"Sorry, we're saving them to put out for Santa."

"Yeah, right. In other words, you're eating them yourselves on Christmas morning."

Adam smiled. "Only if he doesn't show up."

"Sugar cookies and beer?" Monty made a face. "Who does that?"

"Don't knock it if you haven't tried it. Sweet and savory. It's a great combo."

As if Cole needed another reminder of last night with Mila. Once again he was tasting the sweet potatoes topped with sour cream.

The comments about cookies and Santa didn't faze him, though. His thoughts, aka concerns, about Mila had blocked any references to the holiday and he'd mostly ignored the decorations in Adam's cabin.

Since this was his second visit in less than twenty-four hours, he was vaguely aware of a tree surrounded by gifts. Something hanging from the arched kitchen doorway could be mistletoe.

Decorations covered the mantle and other things hug from the beamed ceiling, but he hadn't identified any of it. He was grateful that Adam had chosen not to play Christmas music in the background during the poker game.

Dealing with a holiday atmosphere in the cabin was good practice, especially if he intended to eat dinner at the main house on Christmas Eve and sing carols on the parade down to the barn. He was determined to do it, no matter what Mila decided about tonight.

"Cole? Want another brewsky?" Rio approached from the direction of the kitchen.

"You bet." He left his chair. "I'll—"

"Figured you would." Rio handed him a chilled bottle. "Take this. I'll go fetch another one. Raking in all those chips makes a guy thirsty, right?"

He chuckled. "Right. Thanks." He wished to hell he wasn't winning so many hands. He'd played these guys plenty of times prior to diving into his Beaver Bunch project. Games after dinner at the main house happened all the time and he'd won his share of hands. But he'd never dominated like this.

"I have a theory." Luis settled back in his chair, beer in hand. "Cole *says* all he's been doing holed up in his loft for the past couple of months is working on his secret project. But what if he's also been playing video poker every night and sharpening his skills?"

Putting down his beer, he held up both hands, palms out. "Swear to God, I've done nothing of the kind. That project has taken more hours than I can count. Trust me, I didn't have time for video poker."

"So are you gonna tell us what it is?" Rio's expression brightened. "This would be a perfect time. Nobody's here but us."

"But you're a big chunk of the folks I want to surprise."

"I know, but we're your bros. It would be so fun if we know and the ladies don't."

"Rio." Adam gave him a warning glance. "You're about to get all of us in trouble. If I know and don't tell Tracy—"

"No kidding. Thanks, *hermano*." Luis raised a bottle in Adam's direction. "Jordan's his sister, for Pete's sake. If she finds out I knew in advance and didn't tell her, there'd be hell to pay."

"No worries." Cole glanced around the table. "I'm not telling. And I promise I haven't even thought about poker since the last time we played. I have no idea why I'm winning today."

"I'll stick to my explanation." Adam reached for a handful of chips from the big bowl in the middle of the table. "Now that Mila's in his life, he's golden."

"Could be. She has powers." Luis gave Cole a light punch on the arm. "In case I haven't said it yet, I'm glad you two are together. Her last guy was a total loser."

Monty groaned. "Don't remind me. That dude had so much baggage he needed a semi to haul it all."

"Then he tried to unload it on her." Zay shook his head. "What a jerk." He glanced at Cole. "I've been looking forward to this ever since the wedding. Took you guys long enough."

"Only because I've known from the get-go she's too good for me." Truer words were never spoken.

"Well, when you put it that way...." Luis flashed him a grin. "You're right, she is. But then again, nobody would measure up to my standards, but I'll settle for you."

"Backatcha, brother-in-law." It was the expected response and got the laugh he knew would follow. Meanwhile his guts twisted into a knot of frustration.

When Mila's ex had arrived with baggage and then tried to unload it on her, that was seen as a bad thing. He would whole-heartedly agree it was a disgusting move.

That was exactly why he'd refused to dump his garbage on her, or anyone else for that matter. Yet she clearly wanted him to tell her everything. Because he wouldn't, she was out riding around the countryside and he was playing poker with her brothers.

What was wrong with this picture?

34

Mila had never needed her *tias* and her granny more than she needed them now. When she was twenty minutes out, she sent a group text to ask if they were available for tea.

She got at least a dozen back, each of them chiming in and detailing what they'd be serving her and how excited they were that she was coming. So sweet. Made her a little teary.

After unsaddling Sol, she returned him to his stall and gave him a nice rubdown. "Thanks for listening, sweet boy."

He bumped his nose lightly against her chest and she stroked his silky neck. "Yes, it helped. Haven't decided what to do yet. but maybe I can get a clue from women wiser than me." After giving him one last pat, she left the stall.

Footprints had marked paths all over the area as she made her way past Zay's casita and then Luis's. Since neither had smoke coming out of the chimney, they must both still be at Adam's.

The sun would be down soon, and lights were already coming on. The bunkhouse, now called the Dorm for Dazzling Damsels, sat a few yards beyond Luis's place.

It was covered with multicolored lights. Strand after strand lay along the roof and hung in rows along the sides. Last year they'd had half this many. Did they have blackout curtains? If not, how did they sleep?

She'd heard about Mannheim Steamroller from these ladies, and usually they had it turned up when they knew she was coming. They called it *piping her in,* as if she were a celebrity.

She couldn't hear it now, though, so maybe this time they... suddenly *Joy to the World* blasted out, making her smile. She hadn't given them a lot of time to prepare.

No doubt they were running around setting the scene, lighting the candles, brewing the tea. With the music so loud, she doubted they'd hear her jingle the bells hanging beside the door, but she rang them anyway.

The door flew open and Grandma Doris pulled her inside for a round of hugs.

She'd been here many times, but she still got a mood boost entering the fairyland they'd created from an ancient bunkhouse. Those bunks had never had it so good — custom-made feather beds, silk sheets, velvet quilts and throw pillows in every possible color.

The woodstove was original, but it had been refinished in fuchsia enamel. Flames danced behind the glass door and five beanbags in different colors were gathered around it. A couple of extras were stacked to one side. Once she'd asked Tia Kat why the beanbags.

"Because getting in and out of them builds our core muscles, darling, and they're stackable whenever we want to dance."

Delicious aromas drifted from their state-of-the-art kitchen to her left, and soft lights illuminated the bathroom down the aisle between the bunks to her right, which contained high-end fixtures, including a marble-tiled shower and a clawfoot soaking tub.

She tucked her gloves in her coat pockets before she took it off. "I've been riding. I'd better wash up."

"By all means, *princesa.*" Tia Carmen took her coat and waved her in that direction. "We put in fresh towels."

Of course they did. A new bar of peppermint-scented soap sat in an ornate dish in the shape of a poinsettia. The towels had a similar theme and were so pretty she hated to use one. But she did, because she'd insult the Damsels if she didn't use what they'd provided for her.

When she returned, they had her sit in the middle beanbag and brought her a generous-sized mug, a red napkin covered in white snowflakes and a plate of little frosted cakes decorated with candy bells and Christmas ornaments.

She sighed with pleasure. "This is just what I needed."

Tia Ezzie came in with her mug, napkin and plate of goodies. "We know."

"How do you know?"

She lowered herself to the beanbag without tipping the plate or her mug, demonstrating that the beanbags were doing their job. "Because you've been tucked in with Cole since Saturday night and now you're here. We're great company, but not that great."

Her breath hitched. "We didn't fight, if that's what you're saying."

"Of course you didn't. You'd be much more upset if that were the case." Tia Kat sat next to her with even more grace that Ezzie. Grandma Doris took the other side and Tia Carmen settled smoothly into the last one. "But something's changed."

"Well, we've fallen in love."

"We knew that Saturday night." Tia Carmen sipped her tea. "Try the tea. See what you think."

She lifted her mug. "I can see you added cream." Then she tasted it. "Whoa."

Grandma Doris chuckled. "We added cream all right. Baileys."

"Did you, now?" She took another sip and smiled. "I needed this, too."

They all gazed at her and smiled.

"So here's what I want to know. What are the most important things to have in a relationship?"

She got the answers she'd expected — communication, respect, trust, honesty, support and most of all, laughter. While they expanded on those, she nodded, sipped her Baileys-laced tea and nibbled on the little cakes.

Finally Tia Kat held up her hand. "We've pretty much run that subject into the ground. What's next?"

"The obvious." Mila surveyed the group. Boy, she loved these women. "What can damage a relationship?" Again, she got about what she expected, the flip side — distrust, disrespect, dishonesty, lack of communication, lack of support.

"My first husband kept secrets," said Tia Ezzie. "That's what killed our marriage."

Mila paused, the mug halfway to her mouth. "Like what?"

She held Mila's gaze. "Stuff in his past he wouldn't tell me, even after we'd been together for years. He was like a book with chapters torn out. I never felt like I knew him."

She rested the mug in her lap. Good thing most of the tea was gone because her hand was shaking. Had her quirky little *tia*, who loved to dance and drink tequila, sensed something in Cole that no one else had? "You left?"

"Had to. *Es un hombre hermetico.* He was unknowable."

"I see." Did she ever.

"I had a boyfriend who had secrets," Tia Kat said. "Turned out he was on the run from the law. Nobody needs a man who keeps secrets."

"Joe told me everything." Grandma Doris laughed. "Even the boring stuff. But I listened to all of it because sometimes there was a gem in that deadly-dull story."

Tia Carmen had tales about secretive men, too. The jury was in and the verdict was clear.

She'd come here hoping for answers. And now she had them. She might not like it, but the Damsels had given her the resolve to do what was in her best interests.

Would it help Cole? Would he see the light? She had no idea. Her heart wept at the knowledge that she was about to hurt the man she loved. Because she loved him, she would feel his pain as her own.

But unless she wanted to live with someone who'd decided to cut experiences out of his life rather than deal with his past, she had no choice.

_35_

The poker party was wrapping up when Cole's phone dinged with a text. Chances were good that was Mila, so he left the phone in his pocket until he'd said his goodbyes. He made sure he was the first one out the door.

"We know where you're go-ing!" Rio called out in a sing-song voice.

He didn't respond. Rio might think he knew, but in truth it was a toss-up. Could be heaven. Could be hell. As he walked down the hill, he pulled out his phone and read the text.

Can you meet me by my truck?

By her truck? Fudge. That didn't sound good. Not good at all. He tapped in a quick response. *Be right there.*

Sure enough, she stood by the driver's side, her parka hood up and her arms folded, likely because it was fudging cold out here. And almost dark.

He started the conversation before he'd reached her. "You're not coming back." Might as well take the bull by the horns.

"I'm not."

Between the fading light and shadow cast by her hood, he couldn't read her expression very well, even when he drew within touching distance. "Still need more time to think?" Maybe he shouldn't assume the worst.

"Not really."

He finally picked up on the fact she was breathing fast. Harder to tell when she was bundled up. His stomach pitched. "What did you come up with?"

"I love you. I want to build a life with you."

"Sure doesn't seem like it."

"Because it's complicated. I love you but I don't really know you. Keeping your past a secret… it doesn't work for me." Her voice trembled.

He gasped at the finality of that statement. There was no wiggle room. "Is that it?"

"No. Numbing yourself to get through the Christmas season might suit you, but it leaves me to celebrate with someone who's zoned out. That's a lonely place to be."

He flinched. He hadn't looked at it that way.

"I could hope that given time you'd start enjoying the holiday, but as for sharing your past, you said the movie theater is closed. If it will never reopen, I'm at a loss as to how we can have—"

"Hang on. Is this a demand for me to dump my grimy garbage on you?"

Her eyes widened. "That's how you see it?"

"That's what it is."

"No, it's not! Sharing your past, the good *and* the bad, is what normal couples do."

"I'm not normal, okay?"

She stared at him. "Yes, you are."

"I'm not, Mila. I'm broken. You don't know everything about me, but you know that much. You—"

"Everybody's broken! You can't get through life without taking hits. I lost two fathers, and that's left a mark. I've made stupid choices, and—"

"Like your ex?"

"Yes!"

"The one who tried to load you up with his baggage?"

"More or less, but he—"

"And now you're *demanding* I do the same?"

"It's not the same. Not even close."

"Of course it is. I transfer all that ugliness to you so you can carry it around and I can feel better. What a selfish—"

"It's not selfish, damn it! It's how you'll heal!"

"At your expense!"

"I love you, you idiot. What do you think love is?"

"Damned if I know."

"It's sharing each other's pain!"

He mirrored her stance, crossing his arms over his chest. "Not in my world."

Sighing, she shoved her hands in her coat pockets and glanced away. "You're nothing like my ex. He set out to rope me in. You never would."

"You've got that right."

She met his gaze. "But don't you see? You're not protecting me. You're *overprotecting* me. As if I'm not strong. As if I can't handle—"

"I didn't say that."

"Not in so many words, but I get the message."

He swallowed.

"You don't trust me."

"I *do* trust you. It's me. I don't fudging trust myself!"

Her breath hitched. "Then that's where you could start. Goodnight, Cole." Turning, she walked toward the cheerful Christmas lights strung over the archways of the mini-hacienda.

He watched her go, his heart in shreds. The sorrow in her eyes as she said goodbye would haunt him until the day he died. He'd failed her.

36

"What did you do?" Claudie pounced on her the minute she came through the door. "I was watching out the window! Don't tell me you broke up with that beautiful man."

"I had to." She sounded like a mating bullfrog. "I had to, Claudie, and now I feel like *shit.*" She burst into tears.

"Of course you do." Claudie pulled her into a hug. "I'm so sorry. Come over by the fire." Arm around her shoulders, Claudie led her to the easy chair that was officially Mila's spot. "Sit down. I'll get you something. What do you want?"

"I don't know." She unzipped her parka and mopped her face with the lining of it. "I don't know anything except this sucks. And it's fudging *Christmas.*"

"Which is why I'm going to fix you some eggnog with rum in it. But first you need a box of tissues. You're getting snot all over the inside of your parka."

"I don't care."

"I know you don't, honey. But you will later." She hurried off and came back in seconds with tissues and set the box gently in Mila's lap. "Want to take off your parka?"

"Not yet. Still freezing."

"I'll bet. When I get back I'll build up the fire."

"Thanks, Claud." She glanced up through her tears. "You're the best."

She smiled. "I am pretty good at this."

"Let's stay in this house forever, just the two of us."

"Yeah, who needs men, anyway?"

"Not me. Fudge 'em all. Fluffy fudge 'em all."

"Attagirl. I'll be right back with your eggnog." She made for the kitchen.

"Fix one for yourself, okay?"

"Planning on it, toots."

Blowing her nose, she closed her eyes and leaned back against the headrest of her cozy chair. She'd done the right thing, so why did it feel like the wrong thing?

Cole had made his position clear, and even when he knew where she was headed with her comments, he wouldn't budge an inch. *Not in my world.* Stubborn, stupid cowboy.

But he had every right to live whatever crappy life he wanted. If that meant they parted ways, so be it. But oh, the devastation in his eyes right before she turned to go. Tears dribbled down her cheeks.

Claudie's footsteps prompted her to open her eyes.

Her sister held out a steaming mug. "Drink up. It's good for what ails you."

"Just a sec. Let me get out of this dang parka." Wrestling herself free of it, she laid it on the coffee table. "You weren't kidding. The lining is a mess."

"It washes." Claudie handed over one mug and took the other one over to her chair. "Wanna talk about it?"

"I don't know. Maybe. Yes. You must think I'm insane. He's a great guy."

"Not great enough if you just kicked him to the curb."

She winced. "I did. He's gonna be miserable."

"Do you think he'll skip Christmas dinner?"

"Who knows?" She longed to tell Claudie about his issues with Christmas, but she wouldn't. She'd promised. Holding the mug in both hands, she took a sip. "Nice. Does rum go okay with Baileys?"

"*What?*"

"I had hot tea laced with Baileys over at the bunkhouse."

"Huh. That's a new combo for them. Was it good?"

"It was, oddly enough. This is better. I don't usually mix different kinds of booze. I don't want to make myself sick."

"Ah, there you go. You're coming out of it already."

"Out of what?"

"Your meltdown. Ten minutes ago you wouldn't have given a damn about making yourself sick."

"True. I still feel awful, but I was borderline suicidal when I walked in."

"Yep. Scared me a little."

"Sorry."

"You pulled out of it. That's all that counts. So what happened, *chica*?"

"I can't tell you all of it. I promised not to, and I'll keep that promise."

"Of course. I assume we're not talking about the secret project."

"Lord, no." She'd forgotten about the Beaver Bunch. "I guess he'll still present it on Christmas Day, but...."

"It'll be awkward."

"Or not. Nobody needs to know we broke up since you're the only one who saw it happen. We'd already planned for me to come back here for two days so you and I could make fudge. That can be the cover story."

"I guess, until everybody sees you two together."

"Yeah. He'll be better at faking it than I will. The guy plays his cards close to the vest."

"I'm not all that surprised."

She took another swallow of the eggnog and raised the mug in Claudie's direction. "Good call, *hermana.*"

"That's what I'm here for. So what *can* you tell me?"

"Bottom line, he has some ugly stories from his childhood. From what we've heard about his sister's experience, that won't surprise you, either."

"Nope."

"I've figured out he had it worse than she did and shielded her as best he could, but he refuses to talk about it."

"After all these years?"

"He insists on keeping it buried. Even Jordan doesn't know the half of it."

"Oh, boy."

"I took a long ride on Sol today to think it through. Then I picked the Damsels' brains on what makes or breaks a relationship. I didn't say why I wanted to know, but I'm sure they figured it out."

"You can't get anything past that crew."

"They're also a feminist brain trust. I came away knowing that even if Cole and I have a lot going for us, which we do, if he won't let me into his private vault...."

"Are you sure about that?"

"He said it again, just now, when he knew what was on the line."

Claudie sighed. "That's a damned shame, sis."

"You can't repeat any of this."

"I won't. I just feel like giving him a knock upside the head. I thought he was smarter than that. Only a dummy would give up a chance to be with you."

"He's no dummy. But he is damaged. And this is how he's chosen to deal with it."

"His loss. I hate that everything fell apart, but I'm glad you took a stand. The Damsels are right. This is a huge red flag. Will they say anything?"

"No. For one thing, I didn't confirm that Cole was keeping secrets from me. But before I left, Tia Kat gave them all that look, and—"

"I know that look."

"Then she said *this conversation never happened.*"

"Good for her." Claudie's blue gaze was steady. "Neither did this one."

Gratitude brought a lump to her throat. "Thank you. And thank you for listening."

"You're welcome."

"I wish I could tell you more, but even getting this much off my chest is huge. I don't know what I'd do without you."

"Backatcha, sis." Leaning over, she extended her mug.

Mila did the same, stretching her arm until the mugs touched. "To us."

Sharing her troubles with Claudie had lightened the heavy weight pressing down on her heart. But that concept made no sense to Cole.

Would he ever see the light? She longed for that, but the choice was his.

<u>**37**</u>

After a mostly sleepless night, Cole was at loose ends. He liked keeping busy. Having nothing to do was his worst nightmare.

Well, maybe not his worst one, but it made the list. Being dumped by the woman of his dreams while also out of projects would have driven him to drink in the past.

Except he wasn't doing that anymore. An occasional beer or two was his limit. Cleaning the loft from top to bottom took exactly two hours and it wasn't even lunchtime yet.

He considered copying Mila's idea and going for a long ride along a snowy trail. But although he'd talked to Luis about snow pads he'd never bought any and he could cause Sparky a problem if he rode without them.

Then he remembered the arena. Luis and Jordie wouldn't be using it this week. He'd only ridden Sparky once in there and they'd both loved it. Nobody would care as long as he got out the tractor and raked it afterward.

He'd done that job several times for his sister and brother-in-law, who'd been crunched for time as the training clinics gained popularity. They considered it a favor. He considered it the fulfillment of a little boy's dream.

Riding Sparky in that arena would be a twofer. He'd lope around that space like the fudging Lone Ranger and then drive that John Deere like Old MacDonald.

Within ten minutes he'd tacked up Sparky and was leading him over to the arena. They'd chosen a plot of land to the right of the pasture and about thirty yards behind the two casitas. Someone had shoveled the path to the front entrance and taken a horse along it, too.

He wasn't the only one with this idea, but he kinda hoped they'd been and gone. He wasn't in the mood for conversation.

The sound of hoofbeats reached him as he drew closer to the open double doors. Well, damn. Either he could put on his cheerful face and brave it through or take his horse back to the barn.

Sparky was prancing with eagerness, so that settled it. He couldn't disappoint his horse. As for small talk, he'd say Mila and Claudie were making Christmas fudge today so he was using the time to give Sparky some exercise. Both things were true, as far as they went.

As he reached the doorway and peered inside, he chuckled. Should've known.

Jordie slowed Fudge from a trot to a walk as she rode over to greet him. "Hey, big brother! Great minds, huh?"

"Guess so. How come you're out here alone?"

"I'm not alone. I have Fudgie." She leaned down and patted the horse's neck.

"Good point."

"Come on in. I've only been here about fifteen minutes. I must've just missed you at the barn."

"Yep. I didn't notice Fudge was gone when I fetched Sparky." He swung into the saddle. "I would've taken a trail ride, but I don't have any snow pads."

"I do, if you want to change your mind."

"Nah, this looks like more fun." She was the one person he could stand to be with right now. "We can go faster."

"That's what I decided." She smiled. "Besides, I like this place."

"Because of your wedding?"

"Definitely that, but also because you built it. Every time I come in here I think of how hard you worked on it."

"Not just me." But he loved hearing that she connected him to this building.

"Mostly you."

He gave her a smile. "So where's Luis?"

"He's working on the sleigh with Rio. They think the snow will still be good enough on Christmas Day to take it out."

"You didn't want to help get it ready?"

"They invited me, but they need some brotherly time together. And I could use a break from hearing about all the fun they've had in past Christmases."

"Yeah, I heard a lot of those stories yesterday during the poker game. It gets old."

She gazed at him. "How're you doing?"

"Fine."

"Hm." She studied him for a moment. Then she glanced at Sparky, who continued to prance. "He's getting impatient. We should do this. How fast do you want to go?"

"I thought I'd switch off between a lope and a trot, but you were here first. Your call. And you get to lead."

She laughed. "That was never up for debate. Let's go." She reined Fudge around and nudged him with her heels. The black gelding took off at a brisk trot.

His heart lifted as he mounted up and followed on Sparky, holding him back a little to give her plenty of room to maneuver. They couldn't race in this confined space, but it reminded him of how they used to on their rusty old bikes. She'd been a scrappy competitor.

He could still picture those races, her blonde hair pulled through the back of her baseball cap like a pennant flapping in the wind as she leaned forward and pedaled like crazy. He hadn't let her win every time, but a lot of the time.

Watching Fudge circling the arena was a pleasure, too. Thanks to Monty's doctoring, he'd completely recovered from the hoof abscess he'd developed in July. Having a vet in the family was a big perk of living at Laughing Creek Ranch.

Hell, there were so many perks he couldn't count them all. Like today for instance, he had the privilege of hanging out with Jordie while riding a great horse he'd been given by her generous husband.

A few days ago his future had sparkled with promise. But now the magic was slipping through his fingers and he didn't know how to stop it from happening.

They rode without trying to talk over the echo of pounding hooves on the sandy surface. The steady rhythm of the horse under him didn't require his full attention, which gave him plenty of time to think about Mila's clear challenge.

Did she understand what she'd asked of him? And how things would change if he complied?

But they'd already changed and he couldn't see a way back to what he'd had. The thought of giving her what she wanted made his stomach pitch. He might break down. She'd never see him the same way again.

But if he continued to refuse, he'd lose her. Could he stand to live here, knowing she was only steps away, knowing he could run into her at any moment?

On the flip side, could he stand to leave? What about Jordie and this family he'd grown to love? What about Sparky? Even if Luis let him take the horse, he'd have no business doing that.

He'd have to say goodbye to the loft he'd created. And the Beaver Bunch. He could teach someone to run the program, but would they even want that display? Everything he'd built here — the relationships, the loft, the animatronics, even this arena would be lost to him.

He went over it again and again, getting no answers but unable to escape his spiraling thoughts.

"Ready to call it?"

He dragged himself out of the pit of despair he was drowning in. "You bet!" His voice sounded strained to him. Hopefully not to her. He slowed Sparky to a trot.

"We should walk them around a few times."

"Right."

She turned in her saddle. "You don't have to stay back there."

"Right." His vocabulary seemed to be shrinking along with his prospects. He guided Sparky up next to Fudge.

"Okay, what's wrong?"

He glanced at her and couldn't come up with what to say.

"It's Mila, isn't it?"

He nodded.

"Is she upset because you're not into Christmas?"

"Not exactly." He cleared his throat. "She doesn't like..." He cleared it again. "How I deal with it."

"How do you deal with it?"

"I block it out."

Her eyes widened. "How long have you been doing that?"

"A long time."

"Oh, Cole."

He sucked in a breath. "It works, damn it."

"Could you break that habit?"

"Don't know."

"Well, you need to. I can see why it would bother her."

He sighed. "I...yeah, I could break it. Wouldn't be easy, but... I'd give it a shot." He took another breath. "But that's not all."

"Oh."

"She wants to hear about...." He made a vague gesture. "Everything."

Her breathing hitched.

"Yeah."

"And you don't want to tell her."

"Right."

"That sounds like you."

He glanced at her. She was looking at him with such kindness that his throat closed up.

"Cole, you need to talk to her."

"But I—"

"I know it's hard. I know you don't want to."

"Jordie, you don't—"

"I didn't want to, either. I tried to convince Luis it was pointless."

"You told him?"

"I did. And so should you."

He shook his head. "It's so ugly. I don't want anybody to hear it, most of all her."

"She's not just anybody. She's Mila, the one you're supposed to be with, the one who will understand. She needs to know you, all of you, or it'll never work."

"That's what she said."

"That's what Luis said, too."

"When?"

"Back in September, when we were planning the wedding. He asked me to tell him everything. It was important to him, so I forced myself to do it."

"And?"

"I've never felt so much relief in my life. It was important to *me.* Later he confessed that if I'd refused, he would have called off the wedding."

"No, he wouldn't. He loves you so much that he—"

"Oh, I think he would have. Mila loves you very much, too. That's why she's asking this."

Heart thumping, he met her gaze. "I'll think about it." He knew his sister's story, and if he had a similar one....

But he didn't. Even she didn't know that. He couldn't imagine unloading the truth on Mila and watching her face as she absorbed it. How could he ask the woman he loved to share his nightmare?

When the horses were cooled down, Jordie made him a deal. Since he loved driving the tractor and she didn't much care for it, she'd take the horses back and unsaddle them while he raked the arena.

Consequently he had even more time to think. The task had a Zen quality, like a giant version of a tabletop rock garden. First he slowly raked down the middle. Then he started on the outside and drove in concentric ovals, creating a neat pattern of grooves in the sand.

As he drove, he came up with a partial solution to his problem. It wasn't what Mila had asked for and he wasn't sure he could do it. The idea gave him cold chills.

But with his back against the wall, he had no choice but to act.

38

Mila wasn't counting on Cole showing up for Christmas dinner but she hadn't mentioned that to anyone except Claudie. Their mom had included him in the head count, and everyone had arrived except for Jordan, Luis and Cole.

The scene was typical — Christmas music playing in the background amid organized chaos as they added leaves to the table, brought in the extra chairs and arranged place settings.

Space was at a premium in the dining room, especially since they'd welcomed Tracy, her parents, Jordan and Cole into their midst. But her family was used to making room.

Claudie was staying close, clearly ready to be supportive no matter which way it went. She'd been a rock for the past two days and Mila wouldn't have made it through without her.

Their mom and Greta were aware she'd been staying at the mini-hacienda with Claudie, ostensibly to make fudge. They hadn't asked any questions, thank goodness. Christmas Eve dinner was special and she didn't want her private drama messing with it.

But the suspense of not knowing if Cole would come to dinner was driving her nuts. The sound of the front door opening sent her heart rate into overdrive. She glanced at Claudie, who moved to her side as Rio hurried out to the hallway.

"The baby daddy and baby momma are here at last!" he called out. "Hey, Mila, your sweetie finally made it, too."

She began to shake.

"Easy girl." Claudie squeezed her shoulder. "Take a breath."

She did, but she couldn't control the shaking as he walked into the dining room and made his way straight to her, his gaze intent.

"Hey, there. Missed you."

"Missed you, too." She barely got it out as the glow in his gray eyes, the aroma of his aftershave and the sound of his breathing turned her inside out.

"You look wonderful."

"You, too." She doubted he'd taken note of the Christmas tree and reindeer motif of her sweater.

"Hey, Claudie." He gave her a quick smile. "Bet you two have been busy making that fudge. Can't wait to taste it."

"It'll ruin you for any other kind." Claudie gave her a nudge. "Right, sis?"

"Yep." Mila gulped. Claudie wasn't talking about fudge.

Cole nodded. "I'm sure that's true." He glanced around, taking in the Christmas-themed tablecloth and napkins, the ornaments hanging from the chandelier and the lighted tapers in red, white and green. "Everything looks great."

She blinked. Was he faking that appreciation? If so, he'd done a damned good job. Anyone would think he'd been consciously admiring the festive arrangement.

"Time to get started." Her mom waved them toward the kitchen doorway. "Grab your food and beverage of choice."

Claudie made sure to stick with Mila as the line formed. So did Cole. When they took their seats, he claimed the right side and Claudie sat on the left.

At the head of the table, their mom tapped her glass. "Here's to all the blessings we've received since last Christmas. Tracy and her folks were always considered family, but now it's official. We were also gifted with Jordan and Cole, and before you know it, Liberty will be making an appearance. To the Bridger Bunch!"

"To the Bridger Bunch!" Everyone clinked glasses with whoever they could reach.

For Mila, that was Rio across from her, plus Claudie and Cole on either side. Rio was flanked by Tia Kat, who sat across from Cole, and Tia Ezzie on his other side.

Tia Kat tapped Cole's glass and smiled. "Nice shirt."

"Thanks. It's on loan from Luis."

Mila glanced at him. "It is? I don't recognize it." She'd paid more attention to the man than the shirt, a yoked Western style in white. She took another look. Were those small holly sprigs across the back of the yoke? And one on the tip of the collar?

"Jordie bought him two so he'd have a choice of which one he wanted for tonight. He let me wear the other one."

"Looks terrific on you." Tia Kat nodded in approval.

"Thanks."

Mila was stunned that he'd voluntarily worn a Christmas-themed shirt. "Yes, it does."

"Glad you like it."

Claudie tapped her ankle with the toe of her boot to get her attention and then gave her a covert thumbs-up.

She took a quick breath. Did she dare hope he was moving toward the light?

Her family certainly was. Last year's dinner they'd struggled to bring the good cheer. Not tonight. Conversation was lively, jokes flew and toasts multiplied. Speculation continued about what Cole's surprise would turn out to be.

He participated in all the discussions. She saw no indication he was either freaking out or zoning out. Every time he looked at her he was fully present.

By the end of the meal she was tingling with anticipation. He was different. Completely focused. That was sexy as hell.

After the group helped clear the dishes, Greta passed out little bags of cut-up apples, carrots, and sugar cubes. Coats and hats on, they filed outside, their mother in the lead.

Her mom was also the one who chose the carol. "Okay, everyone, we'll do *Silent Night.*" As she sang the first few words and began walking toward the barn with Greta, everyone joined in and formed a loose procession behind them.

Once again, Mila found herself with the same companions, Claudie and Cole. Technically she'd heard Cole sing on some of the numbers by the Beaver Bunch, but she'd had trouble separating his voice from the others.

She wouldn't have trouble anymore. His deep baritone thrilled her. She could listen to it forever as they strolled under a sky glittering with stars. She was sorry that the walk was so short.

The horses weren't sorry. Their eager knickers and whinnies could be heard from several yards away, making everyone laugh.

The song lasted just long enough to end at the barn where the group separated to pass out their treats. Sol's stall was nowhere near Sparky's, darn it.

Cole leaned toward her as they walked in. "Please meet me at the foot of the stairs after we go back outside. I have something for you."

Her breath caught. "All right." No doubt Claudie had picked up on that request.

Her horse Pickles was in the stall right next to Sol's. Claudie had brought a small dill pickle to add to her bag since that was what the gelding preferred, even over sugar cubes.

Mila loved on Sol as she slowly doled out his treats and Claudie did the same with Pickles. Then Claudie edged a little closer to Mila and lowered her voice. "I think he got the message."

"Maybe."

"He's giving you a gift. That's significant."

"Who knows?"

"I'll just peel off when we get to the steps and assume you'll be going up to the loft."

"He didn't exactly invite me."

"No, but it's logical that he will."

"I guess." She tried not to get excited about the possibility. And failed. Claudie thought he was changing. She wanted to believe it, too.

By the time she and Claudie left the barn, she welcomed the cold air on her cheeks. She was on fire.

Cole was nowhere in sight. Following tradition, everyone was heading off to their respective homes and calling out their goodnights. She and Claudie did the same.

Cole met them as they neared the step

"Don't worry, Cole," Claudie said as she continued walking. "I'm going home. Have a good night."

"You, too." Standing with his hands in his pockets, he faced her. "I want so much to kiss you, but I'm not gonna."

"Probably better." She longed for his kiss and his strong arms wrapped around her. But although he'd shown evidence of change, the problem still stood between them.

He pulled a wrapped package from his coat pocket. It was about the size and shape of a cell phone. "This isn't exactly what you asked for, but...." He took another breath. "It's what I can do."

Her expectation of being invited up to the loft slowly dissipated and she gazed at him in confusion. "I didn't ask for a Christmas present." She'd bought one for him but had decided days ago it was a bad idea considering his attitude about the holiday.

"It's not a Christmas present. Well, maybe it is, in a way. I've spent hours debating whether to give it to you. It might not help. It might make things worse."

"Is that even possible?"

"Always."

"What in hell is in that package?"

"Something I've kept for a long time. Couldn't quite bring myself to destroy it. God only knows why." He held it out. "Now it's yours."

She took it. In the light from the top of the stairs she could see it was wrapped in crinkled brown paper, the kind that was used in packing. "I feel like I'm holding a ticking time bomb."

"You're not wrong."

"Should I open it now?"

"No. In fact, please don't open it in front of Claudie."

"All right." She tucked it in her pocket. "Why are you wearing one of Luis's Christmas shirts?"

"Jordie brought it over today as part of her program."

"Oh?"

"She's teaching me to handle Christmas without zoning out."

Her heart leaped. "Yeah?"

"Yeah." He gave her a crooked grin. "How am I doing?"

"Awesome." She stepped closer. "Now I want to kiss *you*."

"And I want you to, but more than that I want you to go home and open that package. I need to know if...." He sucked in a breath. Then he shook his head. "Please take it home before I change my mind and ask for it back."

"Okay." Placing a kiss on the tips of her fingers, she pressed them against his mouth.

He closed his eyes.

"I love you." Turning, she hurried toward the colorful lights of the mini-hacienda. Her sister would be curious about the gift.

In the end she convinced Claudie it was highly personal and not to be shared. She hinted it might be sloppy love poems. For all she knew it was.

Except it wasn't. The small and cheaply made notebook began with a sentence in pencil by someone who had just learned to write.

There was a date at the top. On Christmas Day twenty-eight years ago, Cole had written in all caps. I HATE XMAS!!! The page was dimpled, either with drops of water... or tears.

As she slowly turned the pages, the notes got longer, took up more pages and had less dimpled places and more harsh words. Each was composed on Christmas Day.

The picture became clear. Every Christmas Eve, his father had treated himself to a bottle of Wild Turkey. Then he'd invited his son to the tool shed for a man-to-man *talk*.

The last entry was dated twenty years ago, the first and only time his father had drawn blood. That day, pressing hard enough to pierce the paper as he wrote, he'd vowed to get strong enough to fight back.

39

Cole hadn't truly slept since Mila had left on Monday. Theoretically he should be wired, caught up in speculation about her reaction to his notebook.

Instead he flipped off the lights, shucked his clothes and climbed into bed. He'd done his best to fix the problems he'd created. The next move was hers.

He woke from the deepest sleep he'd had in ages. Gray light filtered in through the windows. Christmas morning. First time in years he hadn't been hung over on this day.

Stretching, he turned over. And froze.

Mila, a very naked and delicious looking Mila, was in his bed. Smiling at him. "Merry Christmas, Cole."

"This better not be a dream."

"It's not a dream." She traced his lips with the tip of her finger. "I've been here all night."

"All *night*? Does Claudie know you're here?"

"I left her a note and came up around ten, thinking we could talk, and all the lights were off. I was afraid you might be sitting in the dark, worrying about us. Clearly that wasn't the case."

"I *was* worried about us. But I haven't been sleeping much, and after I gave you that notebook I just sort of crashed."

"I'm glad you got a good night's sleep. So did I."

"I still can't believe you've been here all night. Why didn't you wake me up?"

"Because you needed the rest and because I love you." She ran her finger over his eyebrows. "I love your bushy eyebrows and your long lashes and the slope of your nose and your amazingly soft beard. Most of all I love your mouth."

"That all sounds like a good reason to make your presence known when you climbed into my bed last night."

"Whose bed?"

"My...." He gazed at her. "*Our* bed?"

"It has a nice ring to it. And speaking of rings, I notice you're not wearing one."

"I never saw the point." Then he clued in to where she was headed. "Neither are you."

"Not yet." She batted her eyelashes at him.

"Mila Bridger, are you trying to get me to propose?"

"Would I do such a thing?"

"No, you would not, and that's why I'm thinking this really is a dream. You've made it clear you don't know me well enough. I haven't told you all the details of my past. That notebook was my lame attempt to give you at least some background, but—"

"Did you beat him up the next Christmas Eve?"

For a moment the old rage burned in his chest, hot and fierce. As he gazed at Mila, it slowly faded. "Yes, I did."

"Good."

"He never touched me again."

She cupped his cheek. "I know you well enough, *mi amor.* I know you're strong and brave and a survivor. I could search the world and never find someone I could love the way I love you."

Damn, this was a dream, after all. Two days ago he wouldn't have given himself a chance in hell. And now she was making him sound like a fudging hero.

"Your only flaw, *mi amor*, is that you're a little slow on the uptake, so I'll just do it myself. Cole Sterling, will you marry me?"

"Come here." He hauled her in close. She felt real, but that didn't necessarily prove anything.

"What's your answer? Yes or no?"

"You're talking nonsense, so I'm trying to figure out if you're real or not."

"Oh, for pity's sake." Grabbing his face, she kissed him.

Not just a peck on the cheek, either. She *really* kissed him, to the point that he rolled her to her back and yanked open the drawer where the condoms lived. He was a responsible guy, even during dream sex.

Suiting up quickly, he checked to make sure Mila was still his dream lover who supposedly wanted to marry him. Yep, still Mila, her cheeks flushed and her dark eyes bright.

He sank into her warmth with a sigh of pleasure, figuring this was the moment when he'd wake up. But he didn't. As he began to stroke, as she rose to meet him, her body eager for his, it gradually occurred to him that he could be wrong. This might be real.

When she tightened around his cock and his climax hovered near, he became more convinced. The details were too perfect — her dark hair splayed across the pillow, her arms wrapped around him, the jubilation in her cries as she came, the thunder in his body as he followed her over the edge.

Propped above her, his chest heaving as he caught his breath, he looked into her eyes. "You're real."

"Yes, you crazy cowboy. Are you gonna marry me or not?"

"Hell, yeah." He gulped in more air. "I can't believe you're making that offer, but only a fudging fool would turn it down."

"Then it's settled. Let's make it soon."

"Very soon." The glow in her eyes filled him with an emotion that was almost too big to fit in his chest. Leaning down he kissed her gently. "I fudging love you, Mila Bridger."

Then he settled in for another kiss. He'd have to get up in a minute, but accepting a proposal from the woman of his dreams was a miracle. It might even be a Christmas miracle.

<u>40</u>

"I really do have to leave." Mila gave her husband-to-be another kiss as they snuggled in bed after making love one more time. "I'm not going to greet my family on Christmas morning in the clothes I wore last night."

"Then give me ten minutes to shower and put something on so I can come with you. I'm not letting you out of my sight."

"Do you still think you're dreaming?"

"Yes, ma'am. If you'd spent every Christmas of your life the way I have, you'd think so, too."

Her heart wrenched. "It's real." She hugged him tight, wishing she could squeeze out all the bad memories. "I love you so much."

"I can tell. I can barely breathe."

"Sorry!" Laughing, she let him go.

He sucked in air. "You're a lot stronger than you look."

"I'm a ranch girl."

He smiled. "Just what I always wanted."

"Well, you've got one. Now go take that shower, cowboy, so we can head over."

"Ranch girls are bossy." Giving her a wink, he left the bed and walked toward the bathroom.

"I'll text Claudie. We'll grab breakfast while we're there."

"Sounds good."

She watched him go. So powerful. So brave. So beautiful. Now that she knew what to look for, she could see those scars, even from a distance. His badge of honor.

Tears blurred her view. She'd cried after reading his notebook, but she'd worked hard not to cry since coming over here. Knowing him, he'd blame himself for her tears.

While he showered, she retrieved the clothes she'd carefully taken off last night after she'd crept into his dark bedroom. She'd slowly climbed under the covers, determined not to wake him.

Normally being in bed with a naked Cole turned her on, but last night she'd simply wanted to be there, to be close, to listen to his relaxed breathing as he slept.

The depth of his sleep had calmed her. Perhaps giving her that notebook had already helped. He'd tell her more about his childhood eventually. She had no doubt of that. But today wasn't for raking the ashes of the past. Today they'd celebrate their joyous future.

While he dressed, she made up the bed.

"You don't have to do that."

"Why not? It's my bed, too, and it keeps my hands busy."

He laughed. "I like hearing that. It also sounds like you might be moving in soon."

"That's my plan."

"Will Claudie be sad?"

How like him to worry about that. "A little, but our office is there. We'll see each other almost every day."

"That's true." He fastened the snaps on a green Western shirt.

"That shirt looks good on you." But then everything did.

He tucked it into his jeans. "It's as close to Christmas colors as I have."

She paused, her gaze meeting his. "I love that you even thought about it."

"You want to marry me. If it makes you happy, I'll wear the ugliest Christmas sweater ever made."

If any other man had said that, she'd respond with a joke. But for this guy it was no laughing matter. Tossing a pillow on the bed, she crossed the room, wrapped her arms around his neck and kissed him.

With a groan, he drew her against his solid body and kissed her back, surrounding her with warmth, with love, with joy. She grew dizzy with the sheer force of it. She never wanted to leave the magic circle of his arms. She—

"Your phone's ringing," he murmured against her mouth.

She heaved a sigh. "Bet it's Claudie."

"Bet it is." He loosened his grip.

Reluctantly leaving the shelter of his arms, she picked up her phone from the bedside table and tapped the screen. "Hey, Claudie."

"Sorry if I'm interrupting something, but it's already past ten. You two need to stop canoodling and get your asses over here."

She glanced at Cole, who was grinning. "Be right there, Claud. Thanks."

"You're welcome, lovebirds. See you soon."

Cole's grin widened. "Like I said, ranch girls are bossy. Let's go."

When they walked into the mini-hacienda minutes later, Claudie was making French toast. As soon as they ditched their coats, she handed them each a glass of orange juice. "Merry Christmas! It's a beautiful morning!"

"The most beautiful Christmas morning of my life," Cole said. "Mila asked me to marry her."

"Oh, my gosh!" Claudie rushed to hug her and orange juice went everywhere.

"No worries, no worries." She laughed it off. "I need a shower anyway. Let me do that real quick before we eat."

"That works. I'll keep the French toast warm. And congratulations, you two." She beamed at them. "Fabulous news. A great Christmas present."

Mila hurried to her room with its attached bath and left both doors open, hoping to eavesdrop on the conversation between Cole and Claudie. She was as surprised as Claudie that Cole had come right out with the news. Surprised and thrilled.

Since he'd been so open about that subject, what else might he tell her sister? But with the noise of the shower and her rush to get dressed afterward, she couldn't hear a thing.

Turned out it didn't matter. The minute she walked into the kitchen, Claudie announced that he'd told her about the notebook.

She glanced at Cole, who was pouring coffee while Claudie dished up the French toast.

"I thought it would be good for her to know. I'm not planning to pass it around. In fact, I'd be in favor of burning it."

She nodded. "Might be a good idea."

"But giving it to you unlocked a door for me. Now I can say it. My dad used to beat me. It's a fact. And it's not something to be ashamed of."

"Definitely not. But Jordan doesn't know, right? So—"

"I'm asking both of you to keep this to yourselves for now. Today's not the time, for sure. Give me a chance to break it to her gently. She doesn't need all the gory details. Nobody does." His gaze locked with hers.

The significance of that statement was huge. He'd provided her with the gory details. No one else. The rest of the family would get a tamer version of his story.

She'd thought that when they made love, they were as close as two people could be. Not true. In making her the sole caretaker of his darkest secrets, he'd bestowed a measure of trust that took her breath away.

That reality stayed with her as they quickly ate breakfast before leaving to join the rest of the family gathering in front of the barn. Claudie poured coffee into three to-go mugs with snap-on lids.

Looked like those walking to the barn were armed with the same to-go mugs along with scarfs, gloves and hats.

Cole glanced at her as they neared the base of the steps. "Don't come up."

"Don't you want company up there while you...." She trailed off before she gave Claudie too much info.

"Of course, but I'd rather have you out there where you can see. It's for you, too, you know."

"But I've already—"

"Not quite. I added a couple of things." He smiled. "Go be my audience, *mi amor.*" He planted one on her and bounded up the stairs.

"Be careful on those steps!"

Claudie chuckled. "I wouldn't worry. He's so high on love he could probably fly up there. C'mon, let's go see this surprise." She tugged on Mila's arm. "I want a good spot."

"In a sec." She waited until he was on the landing before walking away. "I can't believe he told you about the notebook."

"I can't either. He didn't reveal much, just that it was his way of dealing with the beatings. I don't want to read it, but clearly it means a lot to him that you did."

"It also meant a lot to me. It filled in the missing pieces."

"And prompted you to propose?"

"He's the one, so why not?"

"Why not, indeed. I'm over-the-moon happy for you, chica. Who are we telling?"

"Nobody until at least after the surprise and we're back to the regular Christmas routine."

"Gotcha. Hey, look, Rio's wearing reindeer antlers on his Stetson. That's new."

"And Luis and Jordan have matching Santa hats. So cute."

"Mom's wearing one, too. Lookin' festive, Mom!"

"Let's make sure we're front and center." Mila tried to figure out the best place to stand. "I think—"

"Ladies and gentlemen!" Cole's voice boomed out over the sound system. "Please direct your attention to the front of the barn!"

She turned toward the loft and crossed her fingers as a motor began to hum. Would the revolving stage revolve? It had to. Except it wasn't. She held her breath, and slowly it began to swivel.

Soft murmurs turned to gasps and then shouts and applause.

"Presenting...the Beaver Bunch!"

She stared at the display. He'd inserted her little Christmas tree into it! It sparkled away, making the Santa hats even more appropriate.

A guitar riff signaled the beginning of a tune that hadn't been on Cole's playlist when she'd listened to this group. Much to everyone's delight, the Beaver Bunch played and sang *Feliz Navidad.*

Halfway through, Cole came back on the mic. "Everybody join in!"

And they all sang. The Damsels began to dance and soon everyone joined them, dancing, singing and clapping to the music.

When the song ended, the cheering was nonstop along with cries for Cole to come down and take his bows.

He arrived grinning and flushed. He was immediately surrounded and peppered with questions. Was that the only song? Was it a permanent installation they could enjoy all year? Could it be decorated for Fourth of July?

"Play us another one!" Rio called out.

"Yeah, we need to hear it again!" That was Monty, followed by a chant of *we want more, we want more.*

"Okay one more." Cole glanced her way. "Want to come up this time?"

"Yes." She matched her stride to his as they hurried back to the stairs. "You're a hit."

"Not me. Those critters. And the Santa hats."

"You used my tree."

"Just what that display needed." He followed her up the steps.

"Where did you find that version of *Feliz Navidad*? I heard a fiddle in there."

"You can locate almost anything online if you look long enough."

"What are you playing next?"

"I found a good version of *Run, Run Rudolph.* I want to keep it upbeat. Danceable."

"Could you see everyone dancing?"

"A little bit. I have a peephole I can open but the view isn't great."

"Well, we were all dancing, and singing, and watching those cute beavers do their thing. You knocked their socks off."

"Good." He ushered her through the door, hurried over to the control box and grabbed the mic. "Thanks for your patience, folks. I'd like to introduce the members of the Beaver Bunch. Rufus is on fiddle, Buster's on the washboard and Shorty's on the washtub bass."

Cheers and whistles drifted up from below. Made her smile to be up here enjoying the reaction.

"Hey, Rufus!" Cole addressed the fiddle player. "How about playing *Run, Run, Rudolph* for the folks?"

"You've got it, boss!"

Rio's shout of *he talks!* made her giggle. "They're having so much fun with this."

"So am I." Cole hit another switch. When the tune began, he walked toward her. "We might not have many chances to be alone for the rest of the day."

"I think you're right."

He drew her close. "That means I have two minutes and thirty-seven seconds...no, more like thirty now, to hold you and wish you Merry Christmas."

She nestled against him. "I'll bet you've never said that to anyone."

"You're the first." He let out a happy sigh. "You dazzle me, Mila. I can't believe we're getting married."

She smiled. "According to Luis, when you're standing at the altar, it'll hit you."

"Can't wait. And speaking of that...." He paused, his gaze searching hers. "I have a request."

"Anything."

"Can we get started on babies now?"

"You want to?" Joy spread like warm honey through her veins.

"I do. I'm excited about it, and besides, my little sis is getting ahead of me."

"Well...since you mentioned it, I did happen to come up with a good name last night."

"You were thinking of babies, too?"

"Can't help it. You inspire me."

"What's the name?"

"Justice."

His breath caught. "Perfect." His voice grew husky as he leaned down. "We'll start tonight. I love you so much." He kissed her slowly, taking his time, as if they had hours instead of less than a minute.

His kiss tasted of sweet surrender, telling her without words that he was holding nothing back, laying all that he was at her feet. She responded in kind, placing her heart and soul in his hands. She was in safe keeping. And so was he. So was he.

* * * * *

**Watch for book four in
the Bridger Bunch series, coming in 2026!**

* * * * *

New York Times bestselling author Vicki Lewis Thompson's love affair with cowboys started with the Lone Ranger, continued through Maverick, and took a turn south of the border with Zorro. She views cowboys as the Western version of knights in shining armor, rugged men who value honor, honesty and hard work. Fortunately for her, she lives in the Arizona desert, where broad-shouldered, lean-hipped cowboys abound. Blessed with such an abundance of inspiration, she only hopes that she can do them justice.

For more information about this prolific author, visit her website and sign up for her newsletter. She loves connecting with readers.

VickiLewisThompson.com

www.ingramcontent.com/pod-product-compliance
Lightning Source LLC
Chambersburg PA
CBHW022012120726
47898CB00006BA/2022